DANGEROUS MATE

BOOK TWO: SHIFTERS OF BEAR'S DEN

CECILIA LANE

A SHIFTING DESTINIES NOVEL

Dangerous Mate: Shifters of Bear's Den #2 by Cecilia Lane
January 2018

CONTENTS

Flames burst out of a nearby tent in a noisy challenge to the sky. Cole stumbled back to avoid the blast. Water rained down from fire engines, but it wasn't doing a damn thing to stop the spread. They'd be lucky if any of the tent city survived by nightfall.

He twisted around to catch sight of his burn buddy sprawled on the ground and hauled him to his feet. The military man was assigned to him for any joint operations outside Bearden borders. With both the military and Bearden Fire Department dumping water, it was up to the ground team to clear out any who hadn't already fled the flames and extend the reach of the hoses.

"This way!" he shouted over the radio. He made a

full-armed gesture to drive home the point, in case they weren't on the same frequency.

He'd been waiting for a disaster to happen. The military camp wanted to swing their dicks around and pretend like they were serving as protectors for the civilian camps, but they did nothing when given a list of fire hazards by the Bearden Fire Department. With multiple camps up and down the roads leading into the enclave, something was bound to light up. He hated being right.

At least there were extra men for this, even if it meant pairing up with them for a joint operation. The military guys had their own fire teams, and a few of the civvies had volunteer experience. Search and rescue teams, like him and his burn buddy, entered the messy maze of the tent city while the hose teams were still figuring out how water worked.

So far, though, there'd been no one to rescue. He feared his job would turn into search and recovery by the time night fell. He hated losing a life and loathed it even more when it was preventable.

The radio inside his helmet crackled with a new order. "Fall back! Search and rescue, fall back, now!"

Cole reluctantly turned away from the slithering oranges and yellows consuming yet another tent.

The hose teams weren't working fast enough. A deep rumbling over the sound of burning meant the tractors had arrived. At least the fire wouldn't spread to the dry, wooded areas and take over the entire mountainside.

The shrill, panicked cry of a child latched onto his heart and pulled him the opposite direction.

He paused, head rolling from side to side as he tried to catch the noise again. They were near, but not near enough to see through the thick smoke.

There. He heard the cry again, rising to a wail. He started back into the fire.

"This way!" he urged.

"Are you crazy?" his partner yelled. "You heard the orders. We have to get out!"

Cole ignored the man. Someone was still in the middle of the inferno. He couldn't leave a child behind.

His burn buddy planted a firm hand on his shoulder and Cole felt a brief flash of guilt. The human man couldn't see as well as he could. His resolve hardened; that same difficulty would be even worse for someone without protective gear.

He crunched through the ruined remains of one tent after another, stopping to listen, then moving on once more. He was closing in on the crying when another voice added its sound.

He got eyes on the dark figures of the group before they saw him. A mother tried to pull at an unconscious man. Two children clung to her legs, making her progress that much more difficult.

"Here!" he shouted over his shoulder at his partner.

Soot and sweat streaked each of their faces. The man's hands were an angry red, even in the light of day dimmed by fire and smoke. He'd tried to put something out and failed.

They weren't the first family he'd come across in the middle of a blaze. Panic did strange things to people. Made them brave when they should be protecting themselves. Sacrificing their safety for someone else usually ended with losing everyone.

He grabbed the children first and shoved them at his burn buddy. The mother screamed incoherent noises and slapped open fists against his chest. He held her off long enough to sling the man over his shoulder.

"Let's go!" he yelled loudly enough for her to hear him over the flames and through his gear. He could feel the heat blasting off the burning tents. How she wasn't melting, he didn't know.

Quick strides took them through the fire, back the way they came. The route was mostly clear and safe to bring their rescues through without any problems. Still, relief coursed through him as soon as they broke out of the tent line.

Grass and small trees had been uprooted at the edge of camp to leave a line of open dirt. Foam coated the road to form a barrier on that side. Beyond the foam were the emergency vehicles. Paramedics rushed forward as soon as Cole and his partner emerged from the burning tent city.

"Unconscious at the scene. Burns to hands and arms. Possibly more underneath his clothing," Cole stated quickly to the paramedic taking over the man. He vaguely heard his partner saying something similar about the children and woman.

But outside the roar of flames, he could hear what he'd avoided accepting inside. The man had no beating in his chest and no air expelled from his lungs. He watched with trepidation as the paramedics pounded on his chest and hooked an oxygen mask over his nose and mouth.

He hoped someone had the foresight to make sure the kids didn't see their father slipping away.

His bear roared in his middle at the defeat. Cole dug his fingers into his palms to hold the beast back.

He needed to get out. Now. No questions, no accusing looks. There were too many people around for his taste.

Voices fading away to strangled buzzes in his ears, he turned on his heel and rounded the Bearden engine. Calm. He needed to find his calm. He needed to keep to his human shape. He couldn't let Callum down and let his bear rip out of him in front of all the humans. They were there to make a good impression, show they were just like everyone else. He'd ruin that if he lost control.

Inside, he was a tempest. He tried to keep cool and even for the sake of everyone else, but the months of serving as Bearden Fire Chief had worn him down to nothing. He was glad to let go of command and let his brother, Callum, take his rightful place as clan alpha and Fire Chief. But being glad didn't lessen the tension that still roiled inside him.

Cole ripped off his helmet and chucked it at the engine. His bear wouldn't give him peace, and he hadn't saved that man's life. "Fuck!"

His innards boiled with fury. The fucking civilians didn't listen. The military men didn't listen. And now, at least one family had been ripped apart.

Callum and Major Brant Delano drew themselves apart from the crowd. As the men in charge, they oversaw the entire fight against the fire. He didn't need to scent the stinging anger in the air to know Callum wasn't happy.

"I don't know where you were stationed before, but this is exactly why we made those suggestions," his brother said with the tone of a man struggling to keep his voice level.

"We're not here to babysit a bunch of men and women who shouldn't even be camping here," Brant dismissed.

"What then, Major, are you supposed to be doing?" Callum growled.

Delano fixed cold eyes on Callum. "We're here to judge any threats in the area."

"Threats?" Cole barked. "The only threats I saw today were the ones you were explicitly warned about!"

The commotion drew a crowd. Callum tried to push him back into the clan and cut off the problem before it truly began, but Cole didn't hear him. He couldn't see him through the hazy anger that clouded his vision.

"At least one man died today! Maybe this wouldn't have happened if you'd listened to us in the first place!" Cole shoved at Delano's chest.

Solid as he was, he couldn't stand up to shifter strength.

Red crept up the man's neck. Cole didn't know if it was from his words or from knocking the man back in front of his lackeys, but anger coated his scent.

He wasn't worth the trouble, Cole reminded himself. He had to be on his best behavior with humans watching in all directions.

"You fucking freaks probably set it yourselves!"

Cole balled his hands into fists and tried to swallow the insult. Tried, and failed. His bear roared to life and demanded he take an apology out of the man's flesh. Hurting innocent lives, letting others die? An outrageous suggestion.

He turned, eyes flashing gold. "What did you say?"

Callum's alpha nature washed over him and urged his submission. It only made his bear angrier. He didn't want to be controlled. He wanted to fight.

Delano drew himself up to his full height, which was only an inch shorter than Cole. But what he lacked in the inch, he made up with weapons carried by everyone at his back. He already stumbled in front of them; he needed to take back his power. "I said, you *freaks* started this fire."

Cole swung his fist and landed the punch on Delano's cheek. His fingers lengthened into sharp claws as his bear shoved forward. The beast sent image after image of Delano covered in bloody wounds, fighting to keep the bear from his throat.

The man didn't back down. He roared and ran straight into Cole, grabbing him by the shoulders and driving a knee into his stomach. Blow after blow landed. The scent of blood hit the air. His. Delano's. Didn't matter. Each busted nose and cut lip was a testament to the tensions that brewed between the camps and the enclave.

Hands grabbed hold of his arms and shoulders. More snaked in to grab hold of Delano. They were dragged away from each other, and they both struggled to return to the fight.

Callum shoved him back and held a finger right in front of his face. "Fucking back down, I said! That's an order!"

Order or not, Cole tried to shake off the command of his alpha. His bear ripped at his insides and growled a challenge to his brother. Mistake, but he didn't care. He needed to fight something. Anything. Anyone.

Callum dumped more power into the air and forced him to his knees.

"I want that monster gone!" Delano roared into the night.

Cole opened his mouth to yell right back, but Callum snapped his fingers. He snarled at his brother instead.

Callum's voice was low and thick with the power of his inner beast. He forced eye contact to make sure Cole heard the order. "Get back to the firehouse. Do not stop anywhere. You will wait there for me. Do you understand?"

Anger bubbled inside him. At Delano, at Callum, and at himself. He was spiraling, and he'd let everyone see it. Fuck, he'd messed up. He needed to get out of the air still thick with smoke. He needed to clear his head.

"I understand," he said between clenched teeth.

CHAPTER 2

Cole let go of a long breath and slid to the floor of the shower stall. The water ran red from the broken skin on his knuckles. He picked out a shard of tile and let that, too, wash away down the drain with everything he'd been.

Callum was waiting for him when he finally turned off the water and toweled himself dry. His brother had stripped out of his gear and thrown on a fresh shirt, but he hadn't done anything more to wash up than wipe the soot off his face.

He glanced down at Cole's hands and Cole resisted the urge to hide them behind his back. How many times had they done something similar to their father growing up? Stolen chocolate was sure to be discovered on grimy fingers, but they thought they could avoid Pop knowing if they just kept their hands behind their backs.

It'd been years since he thought of that. Damn. He really was going crazy.

And yeah, maybe some of the damage to his knuckles had been done in the fight with that asshole military man, Delano. But the tiles in the shower looked worse and those wouldn't heal. His skin still stung as the wounds knit themselves back together. He flexed his hand; at least he hadn't broken anything.

He worked his jaw, but no words came out. Callum raised an eyebrow, then made a sharp turn. The time for talking was over before it began, it seemed.

Fine by him, he thought as he dressed in silence. He didn't want to talk it out. Heart to hearts would not solve his problem. He'd been spiraling for months, and nothing slowed the disaster. His bear wanted control and was slowly eating him away from the inside out. He'd managed to keep it under wraps, but his outburst at the fire laid everything out on the table.

Callum needed to take him out to the woods and put him down. It'd solve the problem before he got out of hand. Before he truly hurt someone, instead of just using some asshole's face as a punching bag.

The firehouse was solemn as Callum lead him through the living quarters and out the front bay. The rest of the clan on duty wouldn't look him in the eye. They focused instead on making their engine shine after the fire.

But instead of taking him into the woods behind the firehouse, Callum turned down the street toward town hall. Cole exhaled a silent curse and followed his brother and alpha. He didn't know which he needed at that moment. He didn't know which stalked down the street.

Callum led him into the quiet building. It was the weekend for most of the town, and the civil servants were playing house with their perfect families. Everyone except Mayor Olivia Gale, it seemed. One side of the mayor's double doors stood wide open.

"You will sit here and wait," Callum said tightly. He disappeared into the office without even looking at him.

Cole took a seat on the bench outside the office and rested his head against the wall. He felt empty. Drained. He couldn't even manage to feel dread or anger about what it meant to be called to a meeting with the new mayor.

"He's suspended," Mayor Olivia Gale chirped before the door closed fully.

Bearden Town Hall was built to withstand just about anything thrown at it. It had to be when their guardians slept underneath the building. The Broken touched an orb given to them by powerful fae generations ago and that magic kept Bearden, and enclaves like it, hidden from the human world.

Only, humans had been let in on the secret and they weren't happy.

And Mayor Gale couldn't hide her displeasure even through thick walls. Cole could hear every word like he sat inside with them.

"Cole will not be taken off my team," Callum countered. "He is an integral part of the clan, and you have no right to tell me how to run my people."

"Clan business is your business," Olivia snapped. "When he's working as a firefighter, he is my business. We cannot afford to have anyone lose control. Those men on our borders are just waiting for an excuse to roll in here and take over. We have to keep the peace."

"We can. We are. Today's fight was just—"

"Needing to blow off some steam? Cole isn't the only one to poke at the military's patrols. I have reports of our people raiding the civilian camps, too.

He's just the first one to come to blows, and he did it in front of an audience. He's out." There was a dull thud, and Cole suspected it was a fist hitting the desk. Olivia's or Callum's he didn't know.

Silence reigned for a long moment before Olivia spoke again, softer than before. "I was brought here because of my qualifications. I spent most of my time among humans. I'm serving Bearden in the best way possible. That means oversight, the kind of which humans are familiar. He has to be suspended. Temporarily. Until this blows over."

The outer door opened again. Cole thought briefly of escape before he saw Leah entering. Her eyes flashed silver and held him in his place. There would be no slipping away when she had a monster bear waiting to slice him up, likely on Callum's orders. Defeated, he let his head fall back and his eyes slip closed.

Leah took a seat next to Cole. "Never thought I'd be called to the principal's office again," she joked.

He opened his eyes and barely moved his head to focus on her. "Just... not now, okay? Can we just sit here?"

He expected her to get up and leave, but she only patted him on his knee and studied the ceiling tiles above them. His bear rumbled in his chest, but it wasn't nearly as hateful as before.

Leah had slipped into her role as alpha's mate with surprising ease for someone forcefully given an inner animal. He almost envied her. She knew where she belonged and it soothed those who got near her, even if she struggled with harnessing that power.

He thought he had his life figured out. Party and fuck around during his time off. Work like the devil was on his heels when he drew a shift in the firehouse. Everything was in balance and he operated just fine in the shadows. He plucked strings and moved people into the positions they needed to best help his father, and then Callum, for the good of the clan.

And then Pop got sick and Callum had to step up for Bearden. He got promoted to running the firehouse while Callum went to work as interim mayor. That was when everything went up in flames. He couldn't keep the clan steady outside of the firehouse, and he couldn't keep them focused as a crew at work.

He was glad for Callum to be back, truly. He was happiest working in the shadows. But nothing felt right anymore. His bear still wanted to fuck up anyone that moved.

He slid his eyes to Leah again. Maybe he needed to find a woman. Callum seemed happier than ever after taking the woman as his mate. But the idea of going out and trying to get laid didn't do shit for his dick anymore.

The other side of that coin wouldn't work for him, either. He didn't want a mate or a long-term whatever. He saw firsthand how that could fuck a man right up. He lived the aftermath of his mother leaving his father. No happy ending waited at the end of a rainbow for him.

He needed to find his place in the clan, in Bearden, and in the world. And it looked like the one place he still loved was about to be snatched away.

Callum poked his head out into the waiting area. He threw Leah a vomit-inducing smile, then focused a scowl on Cole. "Inside," he growled.

Swallowing his sigh, Cole pushed to his feet and entered the office.

Mayor Gale put her touches on the office as soon as she took the position. Gone were his father's heavy desk and masculine decor. She'd even had the walls repainted to a lighter color. Tiny, delicate statues were mixed in with the books she'd added to the shelves. It was all different from the utilitarian look he remembered.

Cole expected Callum to leave as soon as he entered, but his brother remained. He almost laughed when both Callum and Olivia stared him down. Callum looked like he was ready to chew on rocks, while Olivia remained unimpressed. He wanted to call Leah inside and tell her it wasn't the principal's office at all. Mommy and Daddy were about to ground him.

Olivia herself was an impressive woman for such a small package. He thought it had something to do with her shifter nature. She was a bird of some sort, and that translated into her human appearance. She was thin all over and looked like she'd snap under the weight of her clothes. Her big eyes were something else, though. She had a way of looking straight into a person.

Cole tongued his teeth and directed a scowl her way. He did not need anyone peering into his darkness. His bear clawed at his insides, raking large agreements into his mind.

"So what's it going to be? I'm fired from the firehouse? I can't handle the pressure so you're forcing me out?"

Olivia didn't blink. "Do you think you can't handle the pressure?"

Cole narrowed his eyes. "I can handle myself. I

can do a better job than those humans out there. I found that family. I saved the mother and her kids. All four of them would be dead if I hadn't been there."

Olivia folded her hands on top of the desk and continued to look right through his rage. "I'm assigning you elsewhere for the time being."

"Taking orders from the military now, are you?" he spat. If he could get that asshole Delano alone, he'd do more than break his nose and scratch up his face.

She went on as if he hadn't rudely interrupted. "You'll be guarding a scientist. She's here to research us and the Broken. I have hopes she will—"

"Babysitting duty!" Cole exploded. "You're pulling me from the firehouse to babysit some government broad?"

"Cole, you're out of control," Callum said thickly. A wave of power washed over him like he'd been tossed into cold water. It did little to cool him off.

He pointed to Callum. "I held the clan together while you were playing mayor and this is how I get repaid? This is fucked up."

Olivia stood, though it barely made any difference from her height while seated. Her hand came down hard on the desk. "You are disgraced after your actions today. I can do whatever I want to you at this moment. I am choosing to have faith in your clan leader's judgment because frankly, I don't see your value."

She slid a folder across the desk to him. "This is the request that I've signed off. One scientist, with access to our town on condition that she accepts one of our citizens as her guard at all times.

"You'll watch her, make sure she isn't harassed by any of our citizens. But you will also watch her. I want to know exactly why the government is sending in their scientist after weeks of the military on our border. I want to know who she talks to, what about, anything she does that doesn't seem like it's in our best interests. Bearden and the entire supernatural world took a blow with the fae attack. I won't have something like that repeated again." Olivia shrugged, making even that seem graceful. "And if you're caught, you've already proven yourself to be unstable. How could we possibly know you'd spy on this poor woman?"

Cole paged open the folder. He thought there was an entire book inside. The font was tiny, and the pages went on and on, some with watermarks declaring the contents confidential. "Do I get a say in this?"

Callum shook his head. "This is the only way you'll be allowed back in the firehouse."

His bear roared in his head, but Cole ignored him. The beast was loud enough even when happy. What was a little extra noise when he wanted to let loose and rip into everything?

He pasted on the fakest smile he could manage. "When does she arrive?"

CHAPTER 3

R ylee hid her yawn behind her fist and flipped another page in her research binder. She'd been up since the crack of dawn, even though her flight didn't leave Nevada until the afternoon. She'd been too excited for sleep, and she was paying for it dearly.

"Almost there, Ms. Garland," her driver said quietly.

She nodded silent thanks without bothering to correct her title and shoved her glasses up her nose. Another turned page revealed a simple overview of the equipment sent to the clinic inside Bearden. Or rather, sent to the military camp, then kindly delivered to the edge of the enclave's territory. One person had been given permission to enter Bearden, and that was her. She'd need to triple check every-thing was still sealed when she arrived to piece it all together.

Her driver made a sharp turn and the first camp appeared.

She'd been told about the civilian camps. Her binder even had an entry dedicated to them. They were wild, maddening places full of camp side debauchery. Even as her driver carefully picked his way up the mountain, she could see the revelers crossing the road in front and behind them. Hula hoops and beer cans were as common as signs proclaiming the end of the world or a person's will-ingness to procreate with the supernatural.

It was a shame all new discoveries weren't met with such enthusiasm.

The camps were spaced haphazardly up and down the side of the road. Some seemed to run into one another. There was little organization, as far as she could tell.

"Numbers keep growing every day. When one group leaves, three more are ready to fill their spot. The surrounding towns are having difficulty handling the overflow," the driver explained.

"Have any made it into the enclave?" The car jerked to a sudden stop, and the driver blared on the horn while a man on stilts crossed behind a news van. Rylee recognized the logo on the side as the one of the station that first reported the existence of the hidden town.

"No one is allowed inside. Surprisingly, that's one thing the enclave and military can agree on." The car moved again, and they eased past the news crew.

What came after surprised her. She expected to see more of the civilian camps, with their crazy colors and even wilder signs. But the ground was burnt and broken wreckage lay in piles of ash. "What happened here?"

"Fire in one of the civilian camps. The shifters insisted on enacting regulations to avoid it happening again. Major Delano is in a huff about them ordering anything."

"There's nothing wrong with preventing fires," she murmured.

One of her reasons for leaving the Nevada facility went up in smoke. Major Delano didn't sound like a reasonable man. She'd hoped to run her new lab without any interference or ridiculous back-stabbing like the kind she experienced at her previous assignment. But, she mused, working with the military meant dealing with bullheaded soldiers more often than not. She just wouldn't have the cover of a supervisor to mollify any wounded egos.

She never expected her research career to take her deep into secret labs on hidden military bases, but she enjoyed her job. She was doing good for the world.

Recruited fresh out of university, she was set down into a world of security clearances and nondisclosure agreements longer than *War and Peace*. While other labs were trying to create new weapons, she worked to keep everyone healthy and whole. She'd taken on minor roles within larger teams working to undo the damages of chemical weapons and even speeding healing in battlefield conditions. It was a great honor to be selected to run the research lab in Bearden and report on the supernatural forces at work.

Being plucked out of her lab and thrown into the middle of nowhere Montana was a relief, actually. There was nothing significantly wrong with her life. She was paid well. She had good relationships with her family. But there was something lacking. Something she hadn't quite been able to pinpoint. She hoped that time away from everyone and everything, with utter control over her research, would help her figure out what she was missing. And she wasn't going to find it with Peter Glasser roaming the halls and breathing down her neck.

She'd been shocked to see him after so many years. Then that shock gave way to panic, and she spent her lunch hour desperately trying to stop shaking and get herself under control. She went home that night and submitted applications to transfer to every lab with an opening. Longshot promotion or downsizing her position didn't matter as long as she stayed away from Peter.

The driver rounded another curve and the military camp sprawled in front of them. Both sides of the road were occupied, with a station near the entrance, similar to the checkpoint they passed through when they left the nearest human town. That one was to control the civilians making camp. This one ensured access solely to military personnel.

Her driver rolled down his window as he slowed to a stop, then held out his ID. "Delivering Rylee Garland to the base."

The guard on duty took a look at the ID, then leaned into the car to confirm it was just her in the backseat. "Welcome to Bearden, Ms. Garland," he said politely and waved them on.

Rylee closed her binder and slipped it into her carry on bag. The camp brought no big surprises.

While she'd primarily stayed on the Nevada base, she and some of her colleagues had taken short trips to other bases and camps.

What the civilian camps lacked in organization, the military camp had in spades. Tents were erected in long rows, all wide enough to fit a vehicle down should the need arise. Her driver pulled up to the center of the camp, dipped inside for a brief moment, then drove her just a little further.

Rylee stepped out into the late spring evening, thankful for the door service. She stretched her back and reached for her bag, then eyed the surrounding activity.

There were few women that she could see. Most of the men were beefy giants. She could stand shoulder to shoulder with herself and still not span some of their widths.

Her first set of alarm bells started to ring. She was assured she'd be safe, both on base and off, though she never thought she'd feel safe again. One night in college was enough to fix terror firmly in her mind. Thinking of Peter made her freeze up, just like the night he used that against her.

Her driver opened up the trunk and pulled out her suitcase, then motioned to the nearest tent. The alarms in her head rose to a clamor, but she still stepped inside. Surely there'd been a mistake.

There were no solid walls, no doors to lock. No privacy to be found. No safety. No security.

Rylee spun on her heel and bumped right into a large man entering the tent behind her.

"Ms. Garland," the mountain rumbled, cigar bouncing between his lips with every word. Ugly slashes like claws ran across his face. "I'm Major Brant Delano. I assume everything is to your satisfaction?"

Rylee swallowed the heavy dose of panic that rose in her throat. The man took up far too much space in the little tent. She could barely stretch out inside, and now he was filling the entire thing with the stench of his cologne and cigar.

She staggered back one step, then another, until her back brushed against the canvas wall. Her breath heaved in her chest. It was like Peter all over again.

She tried to focus on his words. He wouldn't hurt her. Not in the middle of the camp. Not with others right outside the flaps.

"... excited for you to get started on the shifter problem," Delano was saying.

Rylee scrunched up her nose and shoved past the man. Her panic began fading as soon as she was in open air. She took several deep breaths and rounded on the man emerging from her tent, shifting her panic into anger and focusing it elsewhere.

Problem? What an insult to those poor people. They were simply living their lives in the safest way possible before their cover was blown. She saw no difference between them and herself. Their lives existed in one state, then suddenly, everything changed. Sure, they likely had something extra going on inside them, which was why she was there to study them, but they were still intelligent people. They deserved to be treated as such.

Major Brant Delano already made a horrible impression on her for not listening to common sense with fire hazards. His flippant reference to the people of Bearden sealed her dislike for the man.

"It just occurred to me, Major. I should probably be within the borders to keep an eye on my lab and properly work the *problem*, as you call it." She pointed up the winding mountain road. "I trust someone is on their side of the border to walk me through? I'd like to get started immediately."

Delano scowled around his cigar. "I assumed you would want to settle down first. The others aren't expecting you until tomorrow."

Rylee tried to laugh, but it came out as a strangled sound. "You know what they say about assuming, Major." She slung her carry on over her shoulder and jerked her suitcase out of the hands of the driver. "Just up the road, is it?"

Delano gestured to the men surrounding him with an air of questioning her sanity. "You really should just stay the night, missy. You don't know what kind of things those monsters can get into." He pointed to the healing marks on his face. "Got these from a tussle with one of them. They're dangerous to everyone around them."

Rylee drew herself up to her full height, which brought her squarely to Delano's shoulder. "It's Doctor Garland, actually. I am a guest of those monsters and here on assignment by your superiors. I will oversee my lab as I see fit, and that means I will go there now, to ensure everything has arrived without damage. I will remain there, to ensure everything stays intact and to make myself available to the subjects I am to study. Now. Am I to enter up the road, or someplace else?"

The scowl on Delano's face deepened with her every word and made her more firm in her choice. The camp had gone eerily quiet with their exchange, almost as if they were wolves waiting for their leader to attack. She didn't want to remain with them for a moment longer than necessary.

Delano drew the cigar from his mouth and pointed. "Up the road. Hope they have someone waiting. We don't have access without them. Cruz, Thompson, Miller, escort the lady to the territory line."

Rylee didn't miss the refusal to use her title. At least he didn't infantilize her with *missy* again.

She nodded curtly. "I'm aware of how the barrier functions. Thank you."

She didn't wait for her escort to assemble. She simply turned on her heel and began her walk toward the territory line. Footfalls behind her were her clue that her guards were following, but she didn't turn to give them the option of objecting to her decision.

Rylee soon passed the last line of tents. A wide space opened before her on the road and she stepped forward. A small glance over her shoulder showed her the escort standing back with arms crossed over their chests. They didn't want or couldn't get closer, then. Fine by her. She didn't want them crowding her a moment longer.

She peered into the distance. There was nothing to see but more trees and an empty road. "Excuse me? I'm Rylee Garland. I'm supposed to set up a lab in Bearden?" She knocked on empty air. "Anyone home?"

Without warning, a man appeared. He simply stepped out of nothing. Rylee sucked in a surprised breath, hands going to her throat and eyes widening. Well, shoot. She'd been told it was a shock, she'd watched videos of the phenomena, but nothing prepared her for the real thing.

"Ms. Garland, is it? We weren't expecting you until the morning." The man extended his hand. "I'm Judah Hawkins, Bearden's Chief of Police."

"Doctor Garland." She reached out and shook his hand. "I'm terribly sorry for surprising you like this, Chief Hawkins. But I arrived early, and would much prefer an actual bed than a camp cot." She pushed her glasses up her nose and adjusted the bag slung over her shoulder.

Judah blinked, then grabbed her suitcase out of her hand. "Muriel's Bed and Breakfast will have a bed, I'm sure. Step on through, Doc, and we'll get you settled."

Rylee expected to feel something as she took her first step into the Bearden enclave. Other than a shiver she couldn't set aside as a stray breeze, she didn't feel a thing. She'd need to remember to write that down as soon as she could pull out her notes and compare it to any other times she managed to step through with a supernatural guide. Was she able to feel the barrier, or was it her own anticipation?

"This the scientist, Chief?"

Rylee jerked in surprise at the voice. She didn't expect to see two patrol cars just feet from where she'd stood. She glanced over her shoulder. The men who escorted her through the military camp were turning around and heading back to their duties.

"This is her, Cullins. I'll drop her off at Muriel's. Let me know if the boys get rowdy tonight." Judah gestured to the car further back. "This way, ma'am."

He opened the back door and shoved her suitcase inside, then stepped aside for her to enter.

The ride was silent, though not for trying. She pressed him on how crossing the barrier felt, how many citizens lived in the enclave, and how long they'd been there. Each question was met with a mumbled, "You'll have to ask Mayor Gale."

Rylee slumped against the seat and let the quiet grow between them. It wasn't long before they took another precarious curve and then started sloping down. The town of Bearden stretched out in front of her, then they were inside its borders.

"That's the clinic. I was told your lab will be

there," Chief Hawkins said, pointing to a building on the outskirts as they passed.

"It is. Deliveries should have been made for me," Rylee said. She sat on her hands to resist the urge of pressing them and her face against the glass.

An entire town, hidden away from the rest of the world. And she didn't care what the military neglected to say; if one of these enclaves existed, she was certain there were more. She wanted to make a good impression on them and the government, so the others didn't need to hide.

Judah drove past the clinic, then entered the main stretch of town. It was a charming place suitable to small towns on television shows. Stores and huge trees lined the street, which came to a stop at an open field. Judah followed the road around the square, then pulled to a stop in front of a sprawling building with a handmade sign hanging over the front door.

Rylee barely had time to take in the name before Judah was out of the front seat and opening her door. She stepped onto the sidewalk and dragged her carry on bag with her.

"Here we are. Muriel's is the place most of our guests stay. Someone will be by in the morning to take you to your lab. Have a good evening, ma'am."

Judah dipped his chin in farewell and left her standing alone in a town that shouldn't exist.

Trying to keep her delighted grin to herself, Rylee collected her suitcase and stepped into the bed and breakfast. She couldn't wait to get to work.

CHAPTER 4

R ylee had been inside the Bearden enclave for less than fourteen hours and she already loved it. She received more than a few glances and whispers behind hands, but no one had approached her with a mean word.

The town itself was like some idyllic television setting, she decided on her walk from the bed and breakfast to her lab at the clinic. Birds chirped in the trees lining Main Street, flowers bloomed around the thick trunks, and everyone seemed to know everyone. She couldn't wait to explore more than the diner, though she was grateful for Muriel's recommendation. She'd been picking at the delicious to-go breakfast all morning while she unpacked her lab.

Even if it hadn't been protocol, she would have insisted on being the one to set the space up herself. She knew how she liked items arranged. Some things would be used far more often, and those needed to be within easy reach. But the actual process of unpacking the shipping boxes was a daunting task.

She was launching herself into the next level of her geneticist career, she kept telling herself as she ripped tape and avoided cardboard cuts on her hands. She marked items off her shipping list as she went. Slides, microscopes, test tubes... check, check, check.

A sliver of what she didn't have slid into place. She couldn't share her success with anyone. Oh, she had her family, but it just wasn't the same. She didn't trust anyone enough to consider them a partner in her life. She had no one to share her worries and her burdens. She was going about her life alone.

She wished she could learn to trust again. Peter had taken that from her, and nothing seemed to put her at ease enough to move on. She tried, truly. But some part of her always looked for an excuse to back away before she made the leap into getting closer to someone. Friends and colleagues were all held at arm's length to keep danger at bay.

The door banged open, and she jumped. The test tubes she'd been pulling from a box rattled in her hands and nearly crashed to the floor.

She whirled at the disturbance and found a tall, dark-haired man shoving his way into the room set aside for her lab. His eyes found her and directed a ferocious scowl her way.

"You were supposed to wait for someone to get you," the giant growled.

She took a step backward and tried to calm her pounding heart. Her hands went to her throat. She forced a breath out of her lungs, then sucked down her inhale. Waited a second. Then repeated the process all over again. But the breathing exercise did little to calm her.

God, he was huge. Bigger than Peter, bigger than Major Delano, bigger even than Chief Judah Hawkins. She was surprised he didn't need to duck to enter the door. Tattoos covered his arms and added to the dangerous mystique of the stubble on his cheeks and his perfectly messy dark hair.

While she wanted to take her time studying the inked patterns on his forearms and his hands—his hands! those must have hurt!—it was his eyes that drew her in. They were storms of grey that hinted at a troubled soul, but there was kindness there, too.

He could have given her a flat, steely look, but his eyes were soft.

Rylee could feel her cheeks reddening. Her panic was fading as much as it possibly could with a man of his size so close to her. And that ebb in emotion revealed something hidden under the depths: desire.

He was a rugged, handsome man. No. Hot as sin. And extremely, entirely off limits.

His eyebrows shot together, then his nostrils flared like he was catching her scent. Of course. He was a shifter. He could smell her.

His frown didn't fade, but his voice turned a shade softer when he spoke again. "You're Rylee, aren't you?"

She nodded, afraid her voice would crack if she tried to speak.

He leaned against the doorframe and crossed his arms over his chest. She didn't think she could touch her fingers together if she tried to ring his arm. "I'm Cole. I'll be babysitting you. I'd appreciate it if you let me know of any changes to the schedule."

She swallowed hard. There was hardly any space to squeeze past him and through the door. He cut off her escape route, should she need it. She hoped she wouldn't need it.

Rylee pointed a shaking finger toward one corner of the room where she'd shoved a rolling chair until she unpacked everything. "Please stand over there."

"Oh, so you don't need to come into contact with what I am?"

"No, because you are so..." She gestured up and down his body. "Big."

His nostrils flared again. She'd have to ask what she smelled like. Could he scent fear? Did she trigger some sort of prey response? She didn't even know what sort of creature he turned into. Her binder of research was extremely sparse on the details of the supernatural abilities she'd come into contact with. It was her duty to fill those in and paint a bigger picture of what Bearden held inside its borders.

Without any other objections, he took a seat across the room.

She straightened her glasses on her nose, even though they hadn't slipped. It gave her something to do with her hands while she collected herself. He was there to help her around the enclave. He could probably reassure Bearden's residents and get them talking. She'd need their cooperation if she wanted to hear their stories and collect samples to study. "I didn't know I needed to wait for you. I was just too excited to get to work," she said to the floor. "How can I reach you?"

Cole cocked his head and studied her for a long moment. She fidgeted with her glasses again, put off by his sudden attention. "You got a phone?"

She nodded and pulled it from her back pocket. He reached forward and slid his phone down the table lining the wall at his back. "Put your number in there and slide it back," he told her.

Rylee peeked at Cole as she took the few steps to the table on her side of the room. He didn't move. A little more of her panic eased away. He didn't look so big or scary when he was seated. Even if he was still nearly her height. She entered her number with fingers that no longer shook and flicked it back toward him.

Cole took up his phone again and a flash of a smile crossed his face. He typed quickly and her phone vibrated before he shoved his back into his pocket.

Easy, little bit. The big, bad wolf won't gobble you down. He's not even in the room.

"What are you, if you're not a wolf?" she blurted out.

"That takes out all the fun of guessing." Cole shrugged. "You're supposed to be the scientist. Deduce away."

"Deduce? I'm not Sherlock Holmes." She waited, but Cole didn't give her anything else to work with.

Keeping the room and a stack of boxes between them, she set back to unloading. He dug his phone out of his pocket and fiddled with it, but she didn't miss his eyes flicking frequently toward her.

Her cheeks flamed after the tenth time they locked eyes. While he watched her, she was busy watching him.

She tried to puzzle out what animal he kept locked under his skin so hard that she forgot to be nervous around him.

Plus, she reasoned, he was there in the room with her. Babysitting her, as much as she hated being infantilized. He could be her first interview. She wasn't ready to start any blood work, but she could dig into the background of Bearden.

Bearden. It'd been pointed out more than once that it was a smooshing of 'bear's den.' Could Cole be a bear? It seemed too obvious.

She pursed her lips and eyed him critically. Bears in the wild were large creatures and thick with muscle. That fit Cole much better than a sleek wolf. If not a bear, then certainly some other large animal. Definitely a predator.

Rylee pulled a notepad from a box, then tugged a pen out from her hair where she'd last stored it. "Do you mind if I ask you a few questions?"

Cole tracked her as she took a seat at the other end of the table, still keeping the room between them. He barely moved a muscle. "That wasn't in my job description. I'm here to make sure you don't get bothered while doing whatever this is." He swirled a single finger to indicate the mess of her unpacking.

"If you're supposed to be my guide around the enclave, then you're doing an awful job. I don't feel very guided," she huffed. Despite his soft eyes and his assurances, he was a big, mean jerk. "What do you do here? As a job?"

"I'm a firefighter when I'm not babysitting stray humans."

"And I'm usually a geneticist when I'm not interviewing rude hippos."

"Wrong. Never met one. Next question." He swiveled in his chair and a light of mischief entered his eyes.

Rylee nodded to herself. She could get him talking, she just needed to play his game. "What is the population here?"

"I don't know. Enough to keep things interesting. Ask the new mayor," he said sourly.

She'd yet to meet Mayor Olivia Gale in person, though they'd talked over the phone on two occasions. She'd have to be careful navigating any tensions with politics inside the territory.

But first, she needed to lure Cole back into talking to her. She could feel him losing interest with that one change of topic. "And there are shifters of multiple forms like elephants, vampires, and faeries—"

"Wrong again. I don't think those even exist. And call them fae. They don't like faerie."

"Right." Her pen scratched across the paper as she made a note to correct what was listed in her research. "And fae, all came through the veil."

"All of this has been answered. None of us were there."

"Yes, of course. I'm just trying to hear it from your own boar mouth."

"Boar? No. Closer, though." He rolled his eyes toward the ceiling like he was begging something above for patience. "Legend has it that the fae were working big, powerful magic in that other place. Something happened, I don't know what. Someone sneezed on the wrong flower or something and the veil opened. Briefly. A rip that zipped right back up as the universe corrected itself, maybe. Only, by that time, we were on this side and everything we knew was on that side."

Rylee nodded and made a note right next to the list of animals she was quickly crossing out in the margin. Closer, he said. In the boar family, or something to do with their origins? "Was it one big group gathered, or were they spread out across the world?"

"I don't know! One place, I assume. That's never been clear. And just so you're not surprised later, every group has their own veil story. It's much like creation myths in religions. These stories have been passed down for generations and lost their truth along the way."

"That's fine," she said. "I would like to get all of them down, though. Do they all originate here in Bearden or outside its borders?"

Cole stilled and tensed. She'd struck something valuable. Outside the borders meant more enclaves. And Cole's reaction seemed to confirm it. "You don't have to tell me," she reassured him. "I already suspect there are more enclaves than this."

His scowl returned. "Oh yeah? Your military, that

can't provide you with the number of people in the town you're supposed to study, knows there are more of us out there? Not sure if they're the most reliable of sources."

"That's why I'm here," she said and circled a single word on her pad. More.

More enclaves would mean more shifters and vampires and fae. They'd hidden under humanity's noses for a long, long while.

"And bites can spread the shifting gene to turn someone into a bear?" Rylee glanced at Cole but didn't find any sign of their game continuing. He looked angry.

"You want to change us? Turn us into humans? Like we're the problem here?" He pointed to his phone. "Rylee Garland, geneticist. Ph.D. with top honors. Gene manipulation and study, with a focus on communicable diseases. I'm surprised they let you keep a job profile."

"There is nothing wrong with you. You're utterly fascinating." She snapped her mouth shut and ignored her burning cheeks. She raised her chin, daring him to speak, but he only smirked at her. "An entirely new species, right under our noses. But there have been cases in our world of disturbed individuals spreading sickness like the AIDS virus deliberately."

His smirk didn't last long before turning into a deep frown. "You're saying what I have makes me sick?"

"No!" Dang it. She really stuck her foot in her mouth with that one. She couldn't help it. He made her flustered. "Maybe AIDS is the wrong—A gun! Yes. A gun is not a problem when used responsibly. Wielded by the wrong individual, and many can suffer.

"If something were to happen, somehow a bite was made when it shouldn't have, wouldn't it be better to give someone the choice than sentence them to an entirely new life? From what I've read, the little that we know, the first few months can be hazardous to those around a newly bitten shifter. And we haven't even begun looking into the vampire population. They have been resistant."

"Biting someone against their will is against our laws."

"Ours as well, but it still happens. In the case of spreading a disease, sometimes a person doesn't know, and then it's just negligence. Sometimes they're just a… a—"

"A real asshole."

She pressed her lips together to stop her smile from forming. "A real a-hole, yes, and do it on purpose. I want to know if there is anything I can do to help in a situation like that. There's your healing ability, too. That can be applied to those who need to undergo surgery and possibly cut down on recovery time and even the cost of treatment.

"But that all comes later. First is collecting stories, learning about you, taking samples to analyze. We need to know just how little we know before we identify the questions that need to be answered. I was trusted enough by your mayor and my bosses to come here. I'm not a threat to you."

Cole cocked his head and scent the air. "Truth. At least, that's what you believe. I don't buy it for a minute, though. There was a reason why the Broken sacrificed themselves to make enclaves hidden from humans. I don't think it's smart to bring them down."

"I hope I can prove that wrong." Rylee set her pen down and folded her hands in her lap. "I was right, wasn't I?"

His eyebrows shot together. "About what?"

"You're a bear. I thought it was too obvious, but you didn't correct me. Are there mostly bears here?

Do other animals live in the other enclaves that you won't confirm exist?"

Cole blinked at the onslaught of questions. "I'm a bear. And that's all you're getting out of me." He raised a hand when she opened her mouth to object. "Welcome to Bearden, little bit. The diseased and the deranged are here for you to study."

CHAPTER 5

Cole glanced at the first name on the list of interviews and struck it out with a single, hard line. "No."

Rylee approached slowly. Carefully. Like a little mouse sidling up to the water dish next to a cat. His bear almost purred at her nearness, then wanted to roar with fury when he caught the scent of her nerves.

He'd hoped those would have settled after two days of being locked in the same room together, but she still exploded into acrid unease anytime she approached him. They'd spent two, long days in an awkward dance. She worked around him, while he struggled to keep still. He wanted to watch her, make her comfortable, and still, she shivered when she neared him and that nervous almost-fear filled the air.

She didn't call him names or look at him with disgust like he'd expect if she hated him for what he had under his skin. He had no earthly idea why he made her so nervous, or why that scent faded as quickly as it entered the air.

She was a mystery. And the more time he spent with her, the more he wanted to solve the puzzle. And the more time he wanted to spend with her, the more he wanted to run. She was an outsider, she worked for the government sitting on the territory borders, and she wanted to study him. She was incredibly dangerous and giving into the desire to get close to her was akin to setting himself on fire.

But that stupid fucking bear in his core, that monster that brought her there in the first place, that idiot beast, wanted nothing more than to let the little woman dig her fingers into his fur. His inner animal was obsessed with her blonde hair and wanted to see how it looked draped across his black fur. He'd dug his claws in the moment she teased answers from him.

"Yes," Rylee said with a firm nod. Determination entered her scent and forced the nervous air to subside. "The vampires are a mystery. You shifters have been willing to speak, but there has been nothing from the vampires. I can't waste this opportunity."

Cole hated every moment he had to spend in the clinic and had been looking forward to starting her interviews and sample collections of other Bearden residents. Rylee's lab was a thing he dreaded entering each morning. The clinic itself stank of disinfectant that made his nose itch, but the lab held the scent of her.

Outside, among others of his kind, he hoped he could keep his bear under control. He needed to keep himself busy, which he wasn't in the lab. Sitting quietly in the corner wasn't his style. He was fresh off working in the firehouse where there was always gear to be tinkered with or the engine to clean. Every second of idle hands translated into a temptation to pull her delicate curves against him. While he wanted to put space between them, his bear roared, *Mine!*

The first whisper of the word settled over him when he barged into the lab. That sense of belonging grew louder with every passing second. Need to claim her and soothe her flighty nature filled him with every roar of his bear.

As much as he wanted to get her sweet scent of

wildflowers and fresh rain out of his nose, his bear rebelled against letting anyone get near her. She belonged in their den, alone. Nowhere else would do. Cole fought a battle with himself. Push her away, pull her close. Push, pull, and find out why she smelled like she fought the same fight.

It was a disaster waiting to happen. Outsiders like her, smart girls like her, didn't stay in places like Bearden. She'd be gone before he knew it, taking her fresh scent with her and leaving him utterly alone. There was nothing lasting to be built with a human. His father tried it, and his mother had run and left her shifter sons behind. Humans weren't meant for enclave life.

"No," he denied her again. "I'm here to make sure you're kept safe. Going into a nest of vampires is not safe."

She sniffed and adjusted her glasses. Fuck, that was hot. He wondered if she kept them on when she slept with someone. His bear raked claws through his mind. No one else should touch her skin. He bet it was the softest he'd ever feel, if she would let him close enough. If *he* would let himself close enough.

"Victor has personally extended this invitation and assured me there will be no problems. I'll go alone if you're too scared to enter the nest of vampires."

"You're not going down there alone," he grumbled.

"Then you better hurry. I'm asking Victor how to get to him as soon as my bag is packed." She shot him a testing look. Seeing if he'd move or seeing how he'd take her assertiveness?

His bear liked that little dose of attitude. Cole wanted to maul himself. He passed a hand over his face and stood. There was no missing her jerk of shock, or her sudden shrinking away before she remembered herself and stood still. He wanted to kill whoever instilled that automatic fear into her.

"No need for that. There's a door here," he said. "Most of the big buildings have an entrance to the tunnels."

He led her through the clinic as soon as she snapped her shiny black bag closed and looped the handles over her elbow. Far at the back, in a windowless part of the building, was an unmarked door that he opened. A set of stairs led into the darkened tunnels, like a stairwell into a basement. Rylee glanced at him, then into the dark. "This has been here the whole time?"

"The whole, entire time, little bit," he confirmed,

then took the first clunking step toward the bottom. Another door waited there. "They were expecting us, you said?"

Before she could answer, the door swung open into flickering darkness. No one stood on the other side. "They want to impress you." Cole stepped through the doorway and waited for her to follow. "They're using their tricks."

"Tricks?"

"Speed, most likely. I can smell that one was recently here."

Her bag swung at her side, whistling ever so slightly through the air coated with her scent. Excitement was there, with only a tiny bit of lingering nervousness. Her heart thudded in her chest, but again, not with fear. She was thrilled to be out of the lab.

"They're faster than shifters? How do they compare in strength? You've mentioned that your inner animal gives you a boost of senses and physical abilities. What do they smell like? Do they all smell the same, or are there variations between individuals?"

Cole stared at her for a long moment, but she didn't give him a moment to speak. It was like she entered some scientific fugue state and lost all filter between brain and gorgeous lips.

He led them further into the tunnels. Doors dotted the path, some labeled with numbers and others with words. Town Hall. Police Station. Unit 104. Vampires needed homes, too, and apartments were built off the tunnels designed specifically for the night creatures.

Lights turned on as they moved. Rylee glanced behind them at the ones dimming back down to nothing. "It's like some of the bases I've been on." Cole raised an eyebrow, and she continued. "Underground facilities, so there were no windows. Lights connected to sensors. Hardly any noise."

"You're just visiting at the wrong time of day," he told her. "They're the sleeping dead right now."

The door at the end of the long tunnel opened as soon as they triggered the nearest light, revealing the tall, stately figure of Bearden's self-titled Vampire King.

"Doctor Rylee Garland, a pleasure to meet you," Victor greeted softly. He bent over her hand and pressed his lips to her skin.

Cole dragged his eyes away and stuffed his fist against his lips, fighting the growl that rose in his throat. She wasn't his. Victor had old-school ideas of chivalry.

A nervous giggle bubbled out of Rylee and his growl spilled out of his lips. He spun toward Victor. The vampire raised his eyes slowly, straightened even slower, and dropped Rylee's hand. Only when Victor broke that connection did Cole's inner bear stop snarling.

"Please, step into our sanctum, and we will begin." Victor bowed again and gestured for them to enter.

The space was built under the town square and located close to an entrance near the Broken. Extra protection, should the town above be breached. The vampires could smuggle the town's magical guardians to temporary safety.

It was as stately a room as the man who commanded it. Rugs were piled from corner to corner, overlapping along the edges. Low sofas and wide lounge chairs sporadically dotted the space. Only a few were occupied at the moment, and the vampires present to witness the first human stepping into their underground territory studiously focused on everything but Rylee.

Victor swept past them and took a seat in a single, ornate chair on a raised platform. The dais was only a few inches taller than the rest of the floor but emphasized Victor's subdued power over his domain.

The vampire passed eyes over his subjects, then addressed Rylee directly. "I will allow you four questions."

Rylee took a seat at the chair nearest to Victor and pulled a pad of paper from her bag. "Please, tell me about yourself."

Victor gave her a rueful smile. "Not a formal question, Doctor Garland, but I will treat it as such. Three remaining. Be careful with them.

"We vampires are creatures of the night. Our skin will burn in direct sunlight, and render us into dust and ash. We feed on blood. Human, animal, blood is life. Nourishment. Legacy. Power. Though we can eat and drink like normal, none of it provides sustenance. It helps to blend in when we go out amongst humans.

"The act of sharing blood forms a bond between vampire and their chosen. I could give you a bit of my blood. You'd heal faster. Any headaches or cuts you had would disappear. Given too much, in too short a time, however, opens you up to danger. This you must explain to your military watching our town. Vampires will not be their shortcut to super soldiers. You'd lose some of your will to function. You'd cease to have any other drive than tasting my blood again. Revenant, we call them. Blood addicts. A living, dead thing."

Rylee nodded like Victor's words weren't alarming in the slightest. Hell, he didn't know half of how a blood bond between vampires worked. Cole thought it was a simple transfer and revival.

"And do any revenants currently live in Bearden?" Rylee's fingers tightened around her pen and frustration entered her scent. She hadn't meant to let that question slip out.

Victor smiled, eyes laughing at her. "No, my dear. We do everything possible to keep such a creature from forming. We rarely share our blood. One must be drained entirely, then feed from a vampire to turn into one of us."

She glanced his way and fixed her glasses on her face. He wondered if she realized she did it when she felt nervous or fell into a deep thought. Cole tested the air. No acrid nerves from her.

"Cole tells me that all groups have different stories of how they came to be, but the one agreed upon factor is a rip in the veil between worlds. Do you mind sharing what the vampires believe happened?"

Victor made a tiny movement that was close to a shrug. "Who knows what has stepped through. Who knows if it was a singular incident or many, though I pity any vampires who were tossed into the daylight. Some say all your natural disasters are the result of rifts opening. Perhaps some volcanic monstrosity stepped through during the Krakatoa or Mt. St. Helens eruptions."

Rylee opened her mouth, then snapped it shut again. She pursed her lips and Cole could almost see her mind working overtime. She wanted to know more but had already burned through three of her questions. She nodded to herself, then asked, "Fourth question. May I take a sample of your hair and blood?"

"Of course. Words were not the only reason you were invited here. We seek to form an understanding with those above." Victor rolled up his sleeve and Rylee set to work. She wiped at his skin with a bottle of something she pulled from her bag.

Cole looked away, a growl rising in his chest. Stupid fucking bear. She wasn't to be trusted. She wasn't to be claimed. She was nothing.

His bear wouldn't settle. His growl grew louder as the scent of blood hit the air. Sharp, not human.

Rylee had inserted the needle to take a sample. Which meant her hands were on Victor.

The bear sent him images, one right after the other. Snarling over Victor's mangled body, Rylee clinging to him, Rylee's cheeks red from the things he could do to her.

Cole swallowed hard and steeled himself to fix his eyes on them. He needed to prove to himself that he could keep his bear under control. He needed the manic beast to see that she wasn't theirs. She belonged to no one in their world. She was an outsider and the entirety of the Bearden enclave would be safer if she remained that way.

"This has been such a wonderful opportunity. Thank you very much for inviting me and agreeing to speak with me. And please know, I'll talk to any of your people that are willing. I can make myself available at any time, day or night," Rylee rambled.

Victor peered over her head and gave him a knowing smile. The vampire didn't move a muscle, not even when Cole placed himself between Victor and Rylee when she turned to place the collected blood into her kit.

And still, Rylee chattered on, not understanding the currents that swirled around her. Or maybe she did. Her tongue frequently got away from her when she felt uneasy. Cole tested the air. Still no nerves, only brisk excitement.

Victor dabbed at his elbow with the gauze she handed him. The tiny hole closed almost instantly and there wasn't more than a drop to wipe away.

Cole stood when Rylee started packing away her things. Interview over. He needed her out of the coven's tunnels before he started ripping everyone apart. Victor sensed it and even pushed her along with an end to the small talk. He adopted what Cole had dubbed his mysterious vampire persona. Long, slow blinks and single word answers were all she was given.

Cole was silent as he escorted her out of the tunnels and back to the lab, where she squirreled away Victor's sample in a fridge specifically for that purpose. He wanted answers from his bear, but the creature had gone silent and still. He watched Rylee carefully. Waiting. Hunting.

Why her, Cole demanded. Why did she matter so much? Out of anyone in Bearden, why was it the tiny human with the ability to burn his world to the ground the one that called to and calmed his inner beast?

He'd watch her, sure. It was what he'd been assigned to do. He needed to make sure she wasn't a threat to Bearden. He needed to lie low so Major Assface Delano wouldn't throw a fit over him being back on duty in the firehouse. But that was where he drew the line. Rylee would be nothing more to him than a babysitting assignment.

"Your turn."

Cole swiveled in the chair he hadn't realized he'd taken in automatic need for her comfort. Disturbing, that. Almost more disturbing than the needle in her hands as she approached him.

Cole eyed the needle uneasily. He'd broken any number of bones throughout his life, he'd battled fires and taken burns, but fuck if he didn't like needles. "What are you planning to do with these samples?"

"I want to sequence your genome and see the difference between yourself and humans. I want to study your cells and see if there is any disparity in structure between yours and mine. You can heal faster; I want to know if that is something that can be switched off and on and if it can be turned on in humans. And if that can be manipulated, can the change itself be controlled or suppressed?"

She slipped into speaking of samples and analysis, using words that sounded only vaguely familiar. Science had never been his strong suit. He was always more interested in physical things. He was at home in shop class, worked better with wood and gears than tubes and slides. And labor kept his bear calm and at ease. Trapped inside four walls without an end in sight made him restless.

Usually, anyways. Not with Rylee around.

She made him feel stupid. He didn't understand half the words that spilled out of her gorgeous lips. Her big, blue eyes held an innocence that demanded he corrupt.

Dangerous, he reminded himself. She was dangerous. Human. Government. There to study, not to fuck. She'd rip his world apart given the right motivation. She couldn't be trusted for even one moment.

Rylee surprised him by slinking up next to him and setting out the rest of her kit. He kept his mouth shut while she put everything to rights, placing the needle next to a sheet of stickers. She calmly wrote out his name without a hint of fear or nervousness entering her scent. She flexed her fingers in her gloves and settled his arm where she needed, all while still talking about alleles and phenotypes and a brief history of genetics.

By the Broken! He could feel the heat of her through the gloves. It sank into his skin and settled into his bones. She branded him with that single touch.

Cole inhaled sharply, savoring the scent of her as she leaned closer to clean the crook of his arm, then insert the needle. Her hair tumbled over her shoulder and whispered against his skin. His eyes slipped closed, and he barely swallowed the groan building in his chest.

Then she leaned back and stared at his elbow. A tiny dot of blood welled. The wound was so small, he didn't even feel it closing. "Fascinating," she whispered.

His bear preened in his head. She hadn't said a damn word about the bloodsucker. She found him fascinating, not anyone else.

Fuck off, bear.

She made the big, dumb beast sing. There was no future with her. No safety. Nothing meaningful would come of pursuing her. She'd be an unnecessary complication to a duty he hated. He needed to watch her closely and find out if Bearden needed to protect themselves.

He clamped his jaw tight and rolled his chair to put distance between them. She was too close. He could reach out and touch her and it'd be all over then. "Not fascinating," he said with gravel in his throat. His bear itched under his skin. He needed a run and it'd be hours before he delivered Rylee back to her room at Muriel's. "Just me."

Rylee blinked slowly, raising her eyes up to his face. Blood rushed to her cheeks, but it was only wildflowers and fresh rain and something sweetly addictive hanging in the air between them. "Both."

Cole's bear roared again in his head. Triumphant. Proud. Ready to chase the little woman down and claim her and warn the rest of the unworthy males away from her.

Fuck off, bear.

Humans weren't meant for enclave life.

CHAPTER 6

"I don't know what this is supposed to accomplish," Cole grumbled and stomped two feet to the left and through the invisible barrier between hidden enclave and her human world.

Rylee followed after him and answered for what felt like the tenth time, "I'm just following my orders here. No one else is allowed into the territory, so the physicists are using me to collect data."

Without any interviews scheduled for the day and pressure mounting from her counterparts back home, she had Cole take her into the woods to walk a small section of the border. She certainly hadn't found much of anything that could be used in her research. Cole wore a heart monitor and she regularly noted the time and his vitals as they approached the enclave border. Border up or down, she couldn't detect any difference.

He could sense a difference, though. While the sleeping figures hidden away under Bearden Town Hall touched an orb created by fae magic, Cole said he felt like he walked through a wall of chilly weather. A sudden shiver went down his back, even though his body temperature didn't drop a bit. And when a police officer back in Bearden disconnected the Broken to their orb, Cole felt nothing when he passed through the same exact spot.

Frustratingly, she felt nothing with the barrier up or down. Her initial shiver when she entered the enclave had been nothing but her anticipation, it seemed. But she was glad to walk to border and test the theory, even if it got her out of her lab and away from her specialty.

Rylee reached for Cole, and a wave of heat flashed through her the moment her fingertips brushed against his skin. She hadn't meant to touch him directly. She'd only been reaching for the sensor that spat out all his vitals so she could record them with the time and his verbal description.

Something had changed between her and Cole, but no amount of puzzling gave Rylee an answer. She spent two days setting up her lab and terrified of being alone with him, and that all magically disappeared the moment she touched him to take his blood sample.

Her fingers itched for more. More contact. More Cole. He was hot to the touch, always, and filled her with a welcome heaviness. The air pressed down on her when she connected with him. While it should have sent her running, she just wanted to press closer.

"How did you get into all of this?" Cole asked, steadying her hand against him.

She shrugged and jerked her fingers out of his. It was an excuse to avoid his eyes. They saw right through her and it didn't make her uncomfortable, which in turn made her highly uncomfortable. She didn't know why she reacted to him the way she did and she couldn't trust herself around him.

He deserved some nice woman with tattoos and attitude of her own. She'd bore him with her talk of science and new discoveries, and that was if she could relax around him and forget her fears and insecurities. He probably went out at all hours of the night, while she preferred a quiet glass of wine and digging into a book. The days of staying out late disappeared when Peter took her life and her trust and ripped them to shreds.

Every instinct in her screaming not to turn her back on the bear shifter, she stomped further into the woods. "I've always been a bookworm, I guess."

"That doesn't surprise me in the slightest." He easily caught up and then passed her, silently correcting her path with his steps.

"Is that a glasses and nerd joke? Just get it over with and call me four-eyes if it is. I don't care. The idea of touching my eyeball to insert a contact lens icks me out and I'm so used to how I look with glasses now anyways."

Cole tossed her a smile as he bent and placed two plastic flags into the ground, one on either side of the barrier. Flags marked the path behind them, too. "Not at all, four-eyes. I meant that I don't under-stand half of what you're doing or why. If I hadn't gone into firefighting, I'd be working as a mechanic. Nothing wrong with different interests."

She was at a crossroads. She'd conjured up a number of images of Cole covered in sweat and soot, stripped down in the dirty yellow pants of his fire-fighter gear. But those warred with images of him bent over the hood of a truck, dirty rag hanging out of tight jeans, and hands rough from work. She didn't know which she preferred, but she knew both were destined to be just thoughts she had late at night, nothing more.

"I grew up poor. Oldest kid in a single mother household type of tragedy. There wasn't any money for college, so if I was going to go anywhere it would need to be on my own. I'm terrible at sports, so I had to get good at schoolwork. Math and science always made sense to me, so I dug right in and got the scholarships I needed. And then I found I had a real passion for genetics and wanted to be involved on the research side of the lab."

"So you're not some military brat?"

"Have you seen me? Do you think I could survive boot camp?" She snorted. "No, one of my professors recommended me and I was offered a contracting job on a super-secret military base. I was there for a few years before..."

She trailed off, words dying on her tongue when Cole turned her and eyed her up and down. She could feel the path his wandering gaze look as surely as he trailed his fingertips along her skin. She was bottom heavy, with wide hips and thighs and not much on top. The quintessential pear shape of fashion magazines. That disparity didn't seem to bother Cole one bit, as his eyes turned hungry. Red blossomed on her cheeks, but she refused to look away.

"Definitely not boot camp material," he teased with a smirk.

Rylee let go of the breath she didn't know she'd sucked in. Her shoulders sagged like someone suddenly released the strings holding her aloft.

Curiously, she hadn't felt a whiff of fear the entire time.

She pursed her lips and trudged past him, following the gentle curve of the markers he'd already planted in the ground. There was nothing to do but continue spending the day alongside the maddening man and try to forget the things he sparked inside of her.

Her foot caught against an unseen root and she stumbled forward. A tiny cry of surprise bubbled out of her lips and she threw her hands out in front of her to catch her fall. But she never made it to the ground.

Cole snaked an arm around her middle and steadied her on her feet. "I got you," he murmured.

And he did. She lifted her chin and met his eyes. Storms of grey peered back at her, churning with flecks of gold until his eyes were a mix of color.

She should run screaming from the man. She

should feel fear down to her bones. He was huge and powerful. He could toss her around like she was nothing. He could cover her mouth so no one heard her screams and have his way with her.

Instead, she trusted him. He wouldn't hurt her. He was a growly, grumpy giant, but some part she thought long dead wanted him. He was growly, yes. Those growls vibrated through her muscles and relaxed her. He was grumpy, sure, but he did it in a way that made her smile and soothed her nervousness around him. And holy cow, was he a giant. Those arms could wrap around her and keep her safe from her nightmares.

She'd left her lab behind to avoid potential trouble only to jump right into something even more dangerous and unfamiliar. She didn't know how relationships worked. Her one attempt left her battered and broken.

No matter how calm she felt around Cole, she didn't want to open that part of herself again. She'd locked those broken, ugly pieces away and built thick walls around them. She couldn't deal with them and she didn't expect anyone else to, either.

She swiped her tongue over her lips and his eyes dipped down to watch the motion. Despite all her objections and reasoning, despite talking herself out of wanting him, her heart sped up when he started to lean in. Her body was on fire, heat blasting up from her arms where his hands rested and filling her with desire.

He was going to kiss her. She *wanted* him to kiss her.

"Who the fuck let this monster out of his cage?"

Rylee spun around and found guns pointed at her and Cole. Major Brant Delano led the patrol and directed a fierce glower at Cole. The half-healed marks on his face made the look particularly menacing.

She whipped her hands into the air. "Don't shoot! He's here to guide me around the enclave!"

Major Brant Delano glared at her, then focused again on Cole. Slowly, the guns directed at them lowered, but none of the men on the patrol lost their intense looks. "That Gale woman put him in charge of you? Is she trying to piss me off?"

"Major, I don't think she considers anyone or anything but the safety of the enclave," Rylee said to the ground. Her heart fluttered in her chest, but it'd turned away from the thrill Cole instilled in her right into the dense fear she hated.

"You had your way in going into that forsaken place, but I can't allow you to continue if this is the protection they give you. You're taking these men with you. At least they don't have claws to tear you to shreds." Delano raised his hand, and the patrol stepped forward.

Rylee surveyed the men behind Delano. She wanted nothing to do with them. Their hard eyes made her feel cold inside. They felt hateful and uncaring. They wouldn't loosen any tongues or put anyone at ease around her. They'd ruin everything she was trying to accomplish inside Bearden.

And from the way Cole growled next to her, he wouldn't be able to keep his cool. She didn't want to replace Cole with Delano's men. She didn't want Cole to leave her side.

The man had somehow pushed his way past her fear and panic, and she'd miss him if he was taken from her. She wanted him around. Gruff and rude as he could be, she liked having him near her.

"No," she said softly. She repeated herself, louder and more firmly than before. "No. They will not be entering the enclave. The invitation has been extended to me and me alone."

Delano ground his teeth together and stomped forward. He leaned down and put his face right near hers. "You don't get to make that call, missy."

"You don't, either. Mayor Gale is in charge of the

enclave territory. And call me Doctor." The words poured out of her mouth without any thought. She felt apart from herself. Where she would usually be a tiny, shivering wreck with a man like Delano getting in her face, she was standing up to him. She didn't know where the strong, steady woman had come from and she was scared that woman would disappear.

Delano reached forward and snatched her bag from her hands.

"Stop it!" she cried, but he turned his big body to block her from grabbing it back.

"What do we have in here? Nothing we wouldn't want those people to get their hands on, I hope. Nothing that would put us in danger."

"I'm collecting data for the lab back home. I need that back!" She quickly recounted everything inside. Nothing that would be missed if she lost it. Notes, mostly. Extra flags to mark the border. Cole wore the monitors and she could download that data as long as it wasn't stripped from him.

But Delano reaching forward and simply taking what wasn't his made her furious and want to shrink back all at once. He was just like Peter, taking what he desired and not caring for anyone's objections.

She turned her head to catch the rush of movement at the edge of her vision. Cole inserted himself between her and Delano, reached around the man, and grabbed her bag out of his hands. "The doctor asked for her things back," he snarled.

Guns once again raised and pointed right at Cole.

Danger hung heavy in the air. Rylee pushed herself forward. She couldn't be scared. She couldn't let anything happen.

Shaking like a leaf, she stepped between the two, large men. She wrapped her hands around the handles on her bag and pulled them open. "Notes and markers, only, Major. This was requested of me by my home lab. See for yourself, there's nothing else here."

Delano gave the bag a momentary glance and then shoved a finger in Cole's face. "Don't you dare mess with me or my men again, shifter. I'll burn your whole fucking town to the ground to protect them from the likes of you." He fixed his cold, dead eyes on her. "Finish your little science experiment so the rest of us can do our jobs and get out of this place."

Delano gave them one last hateful glare, then marched away a few feet. He spat on the ground, then whistled sharply for his men to follow. One by one, they disappeared into the woods.

She didn't move or say a word until the last crunch of their steps faded away. Only then did Cole usher her back the few feet into enclave territory. She shook when he wrapped his hands around her forearms. "Are you okay?"

She nodded shakily. The brief moment of tough bravery hadn't lasted long. She wanted to curl up in a dark room and put herself back together.

Cole crushed her to his chest in a tight, quick hug, then let her loose. "We should head home. I don't trust them to leave us alone."

Rylee nodded again and silently followed after Cole back toward Bearden.

She couldn't stop repeating Delano's words in her head. *Finish your little science experiment.* That part was incredibly insulting to the work she, and others like her, performed. How many doctors had it taken to develop some of the vaccines and other protections taken by anyone going overseas and into battle? How many years of research went into antibiotics or other medicines when someone got ill? There were no overnight solutions to the questions she wanted answered.

But the end of his sentence chilled her. *So the rest of us can do our jobs and get out of this place.*

The words made her nervous and sent her alarm

bells ringing. What job had he meant? They were there to assess the threat. She was helping with that. She hadn't seen anything threatening besides Delano and his men.

She glanced into the woods behind her. She hadn't felt at ease with the man from the moment she met him and he'd done nothing to change her opinion of him. She vowed to make some calls as soon as she made it back to her room that night and see if Delano had orders other than the ones she knew.

CHAPTER 7

Rylee only managed a few hours of restless, anxious sleep before she gave up, switched on a light, popped on her glasses, and opened her laptop. She began sorting through her emails, adding flags to questions she needed to include in her future interviews and more measurements requested by the team looking into the mysterious Broken. They hadn't been allowed into Bearden as she had, so she was following their instructions while conducting her research into the genetics of the supernatural residents.

But even work she loved couldn't hold her interest for long. Major Delano's words had haunted her all night and continued to do so in the chilly morning.

Nothing in her paperwork indicated Delano was there for anything other than surveillance. The United States government, and, frankly, the rest of the world, was alarmed at the sudden appearance of one town filled with individuals sunk deep in otherness. Delano's assignment was to make sure there would be no threat to the people in the surrounding towns or the humans that turned up to camp on the borders.

But the way he phrased it and the hate in his voice still sent a shiver down her spine. She didn't like the implications that she was conducting worthless research and that he had another job to perform. Rylee frowned and tapped a finger against her lips. Peter once again reared his ugly head in her life. He'd caused her to keep everyone at arm's length, and now she didn't have any close confidant she could ask to snoop for her in Nevada.

Still unsure of who she could ask for a favor, Rylee accepted the invitation to a virtual meeting later that morning with some of the team back at the Nevada lab, then shut the screen.

Thoughts of Major Delano followed her even as she gathered clothes and turned the shower up to a wickedly high temperature. Whatever he planned, whatever he wanted to do, she needed to know. Her research depended on it. The people of Bearden would paint her with the same brush if he continued being a huge jerk to everyone he came across. And it was precisely that sort of attitude that made her research so valuable. If she could show that the residents of Bearden were just like everyone else through the interviews she conducted and the samples she collected, then there would be no threat to rail against.

Just like that, Cole was back at the forefront of her mind. He was the bright light during a horrible day. He pushed back on the bullies that were trying to intimidate her.

Cole was everything she shouldn't want. A giant of a man, with bad boy inked across his skin with numerous tattoos. But the foul-mouthed, surly shifter made her feel more secure than any time in her life. He was a lifeline she hadn't known she needed.

He'd hugged her, and she didn't freak out. She didn't know if it was pure adrenaline from Delano or if she craved touch that much, but Cole didn't send her spiraling into panic when he crushed her to his chest. No, that wasn't right. He was huge, but he'd been gentle. It was quick, done and over in the blink of an eye, but it felt right. More than right. Perfect.

Fear still coated her thoughts and made her feel queasy. She knew exactly how terrible the consequences could be to put her trust in the wrong person. She'd been kept awake by those nightmares for years. She fled her safe lab at the mere hint of seeing that man again.

But thinking about Cole, and feeling the heat of the water running over her skin, made desire blossom to life. She thought she'd never feel it again, not after the bruises on her skin and the destruction of her confidence. But Cole Strathorn, loud, huge, *shifter*, made her mouth water.

Slowly, afraid of the darkness that inevitably closed in around her, she skimmed her hands up her sides. Her breath caught as she imagined her hands as Cole's. Up and up she touched, until she cupped her breasts. Her nipples tightened into hard peaks.

The scratch of Cole's eternal five-o'clock shadow would rasp against her skin. Would she like that? Could she see him, smell him, *feel* him without giving into the darkness?

She held her breath, expecting a shiver of fear and contempt to run through her. When it didn't, when panic didn't force her to her knees and bring tears to her eyes, Rylee pressed her forehead against the slick shower wall and groaned.

Cole was off limits. And not just because he was one of her subjects to study. He was a man in a town she'd never settle in or visit again.

Except, a tiny voice in the back of her head whispered. Except that's the exact sort of man she could get involved with. No strings. No seeing him again if she freaked out. She could ease back into relationships with a man like Cole. He was safe precisely because she'd never step in Bearden again once she was done there. She could kick the dirt and any potential embarrassing humiliation from her shoes at the same time.

Rylee turned the knob and stepped out of the shower. Wrapped in a fluffy towel, freshly showered and ready to start a new day, her confidence soared. She couldn't let the dark monsters in her past continue to eat away at the light of her present and future.

Despite the confusion Cole brought, she was glad she'd been pushed by fear to enter Bearden. She didn't want to let fear rule her. It'd hounded her for too long. She didn't know what would happen between them or anyone who caught her eye, or even if she'd be able to keep her panic locked away.

But she wasn't about to find out by staying inside her hotel room.

She was tired of being stuck in a state of in-between. She was Schrodinger's cat, caught in limbo by a trap of her trauma. She was well past the time of discovering if she could exist as a normal person or shrink further into herself.

Rylee glanced at the time. Six in the dang morning. Stupid Major Delano and the intrusive worry he instilled in her. She still needed to find someone with access to documents or water cooler talk about Delano's goals for Bearden.

At least the coffee shop would be open. She'd seen it in passing but hadn't stopped to visit. Perhaps she could even snag another interview, or at least make her presence known in Bearden. She didn't want to be the mousy little scientist escorted around by the big bad bear. She wanted to be her own person, unafraid of her shadow.

And if she could claw her way to that ledge without feeling the familiar prick of fear when the first man passed her by, then maybe she could start to relax elsewhere in her life.

She reached for her phone and typed out a quick message to Cole. *Getting coffee and heading to the lab early. No need to pick me up this morning.*

The sun had barely peeked over the horizon when Rylee stepped out onto the sleepy morning street. She was once again confronted with the sheer adorableness of Bearden. A few hands waved a silent greeting to her as she walked through the town square and toward the coffee shop. And from there, it was only a few more blocks to the clinic and her lab.

The peacefulness extended even into Mug Shot Coffee Bar itself. A trio of elderly women had planted themselves in one corner, and while they didn't give her a friendly hello, they didn't outright snarl at her, either. They darted quick looks at another woman sitting alone at a table and staring forlornly at the diner across the street. Town gossips, she supposed, as they descended into hushed whispers.

She approached the woman at the counter, who hummed and drew lines across blocks in the newspaper spread out in front of her. Rylee tapped her lips and shuffled for several long seconds, trying to politely appear like she studied the menu on the back wall. When the woman still didn't look up, she cleared her throat.

A great rustled of paper and wide eyes greeted her. The paper disappeared from the counter and the marker in the woman's hand colored her palm in her rush to cap. She straightened her apron and lifted her chin in the air. "Oh! Sorry! I was just looking at the want ads. Nothing good, in case you were wondering. I'm never getting out of here. What can I get for you?"

"Uhm. I don't usually get anything fancy. Just a coffee?" She'd never had much expendable income for coffee shops, and primarily developed her habit with whatever swill had been brewed that day by a research assistant on campus. The coffee found in break rooms after she graduated wasn't any better.

"You're the doctor, aren't you?" Rylee nodded and the woman stuck her hand out in greeting. "Becca Holden. Half owner of this lovely establishment."

"Employee! You can't be trusted with the bagels, let alone owning!" A voice shouted from the back. Another woman bustled through the doors behind the counter and set a tray of pastries on the counter. "Stop bothering the customers, Becks. And shouldn't you be getting her coffee?"

The woman then crossed her arms on top of the case. "I'm Faith, the *actual* owner. I apologize in advance for anything inappropriate that comes out of my sister's mouth."

Rylee nodded in understanding. "Eldest sibling, huh? I have a whole passel younger than me."

"By minutes! Older by minutes!" Becca rolled her eyes and shuffled to the big silver pots at her back. "Hey Doc, I can set you up with something sticky sweet to take with you. Or something bagel-y. Whichever you prefer."

Rylee checked the case Faith was quickly filling. She pointed to the fresh bear claws being placed next to some éclairs. "I'll have one of those."

Becca pumped her fist and set a large cup of coffee on the counter before sticking her tongue out at the other woman. "First upsell of the morning, Faith. In your face!"

Faith stood and shook her head. "I'm not praising you for doing your job."

Rylee shuffled to the register while Becca packaged up her bear claw and rang her up. But the bickering between fraternal twins didn't stop even through her transaction.

Becca slashed her eyes to the lone woman still staring out the window, then fixed Rylee with a mischievous grin. "It's a good thing I can't find a job elsewhere. Who will take care of the place when you bless me with little nieces and nephews?" Becca leaned across the counter and whispered, "The scene has been set. Enjoy some morning entertainment sure to rival any soap opera."

Sure enough, the woman slouching in the corner and shooting mournful eyes across the street swiveled her head toward Faith. Faith, in turn, shot daggers at her sister.

"Faith, is this true? You and Tommy are going to give me grandchildren?" She clasped her hands together under her chin.

"Sabrina, you have been warned about bothering us about children. We will tell you when we're ready to try."

Tears welled in Sabrina's eyes. "I just can't wait to see the little babes. I want to hold them so much. Tommy was such a lovely baby. His son or daughter will surely be the same!"

"Nope. Not discussing this. These are business hours. Tommy banned you from the diner because you wouldn't leave him alone. I'll do the same thing, I swear I will!"

The tears turned on in full force. "You wouldn't treat me like that, would you? Not my darling boy's chosen mate?"

"Yeah, Faith. Your own mother-in-law just wants to know if you're doing it enough to make babies. We all want to know," Becca taunted from the side.

Rylee hid her snort of laughter in her cup.

Sabrina seemed torn between indignation at Becca's words and continuing her pouting at Faith. Her mouth gaped like a fish and Faith pointed toward the door. "You will know what we want you to know. We will have kids when we want to have kids. Now, out, and I will be telling Tommy about this."

Rylee followed Sabrina's slow retreat. "Aren't you worried that will have some lasting effects?"

Becca waved a hand in dismissal. "That fight's been coming for weeks and between you and me, I think they're trying already. She's been drinking an awful lot of water and won't go drinking with me anymore. Better to set the boundaries now before Mrs. C goes Old Yeller with the baby rabies." She eyed her suspiciously. "That's all off the record. You work by journalist rules, don't you?"

Rylee pantomimed turning a lock on her lips and throwing away the key.

Becca squinted her eyes and shook a finger at her. "You're not half bad, Doc. Listen, I'm getting together with some of the girls later next week. If you stay cool and can slip your bearbysittier—see what I did there? Bear-by. Baby. You'll laugh later, don't worry.—you should join us for brunch. We like to make Pierre regret updating his menu."

Rylee blinked at the sudden deluge of information and jokes. A surprised laugh tumbled out of her in her shock. Bearby. She got it. And she knew Cole would hate it. She'd have to find a way to work that into conversation somehow. And Pierre. That was one of the restaurants she passed on her way to the lab.

The timid her, the one she wanted to leave in the dust, would refuse. She'd use her work as some polite excuse, but it'd truly be because she didn't want to get close to anyone. Rylee wanted to lock that woman away and live her life again. She struggled to stem the flow of unease and embarrassment, and said, "If no one else objects, I think that'd be lovely."

Becca's smile widened. "Be there or be square, as the kids say. Never mind, I don't think they say that anymore. They should, but they don't. Probably because they're squares."

CHAPTER 8

A repeated buzz by his head drew Cole out of the sweetest dream. Rylee writhed under him, her mouth dropping open in a gasp. Her big baby blues stared at him like she wanted to eat him up, which he was more than willing to let happen.

That damn buzz droned in the background again and Cole opened his eyes in frustration, his dream slipping away. Mostly. His cock stood at painful attention.

He snatched up his phone with a growl that tapered into a groan when he registered her name. He wrapped his hand around his shaft for one punishing pump. She felt so fucking good. Tasted so damned amazing. Sounded like heaven. Smelled like his mate.

And it'd been nothing more than a dream. Would *never* be anything more than a dream.

Humans weren't meant for enclave life, he reminded himself again. And magically, his painful erection disappeared. Exactly like Rylee would once her assignment was complete.

At least Rylee had an excuse to leave at the end. There was an entire family holding down his mother, and she'd still pulled a vanishing act.

He'd gotten too close yesterday. Rylee was trouble and temptation in one sweet package. He'd done the gentlemanly thing and steadied her before she fell. He thought her hands branded him through her gloves when she took a sample of his blood, but that was nothing compared to her palms on his skin. His bear pushed closer and overwhelmed all his opposition until there was nothing for him to do but let the sweet scent of her wrap around his throat, grab him by the balls, and force him to try for a kiss.

And then those grade-A assholes wandered in with guns drawn and switched her scent from arousal to straight up panic and fear. They'd saved him from a lapse of sanity and made him want to kill every last one of them for interrupting a moment with the woman he desperately didn't want to think of as his mate.

He'd give just about anything for a moment alone with Delano. The man was a monster, and not only for his dismissal of the people he was supposed to be impartially judging to be friends or foes. He was a bully, picking on tiny women like Rylee. She'd done nothing wrong, and Delano and his asshole goons fucked with her anyway. They didn't care that they made her uncomfortable. Oh, no. They reveled in it. They had a taste for fear. Mad dogs, that's what they were.

It was only a matter of time before the military occupation on their borders turned deadly. And just like the fire that burned down an entire civilian camp, Cole waited for disaster. He just needed to make sure Rylee was safe before that powder keg blew up in everyone's faces.

"Watch it, dickhole!" Sawyer's muffled shout filtered through the walls of Cole's cabin.

"Eat me," Hudson yelled back.

"Would you both shut. The fuck. Up," Nolan growled.

Cole grinned and rolled out of bed. Trudging steps and a chorus of grumpy snarls filled the clearing outside his door. He'd usually be up and heading into the firehouse with them if it weren't for his scuffle with Delano and assignment of watching Rylee.

He tugged on jeans and a t-shirt, then made his way onto his porch to watch the early morning madness.

Leah cracked a yawn from the porch of the cabin she shared with Callum. Dark circles lined her eyes, but she gave Callum a lingering hug. Callum didn't look much better, which meant he'd stayed up waiting for her to close down the bar where she worked. The Roost was solidly in her hands while Gideon, the owner, was off dealing with his clan of misfit dragons. They were decidedly split on revealing themselves to the world with the rest of Bearden or staying hidden away with every other enclave.

And if it wasn't work at the bar keeping her awake, it was her bear. The beast had been given to her unwillingly by Callum's recent challenger, right before his brother dealt a killing blow and defeated the man. Leah took to her bear with more ease than expected, but the beast still gave her trouble. It was like that for forced shifters, and he suspected she worked herself to the bone to keep her inner animal exhausted.

Cole shrugged uncomfortably. He was used to

dancing the same jig. Hard work kept the beast at bay. If he hadn't thrown a punch or put claws to Delano's face, he'd be readying for a long day of activity. Watching over Rylee wasn't giving him the active work he needed to settle his bear, but the strange little woman kept him placated, nonetheless.

Callum caught his eyes and grinned. "Aww, look everyone. Someone lost a little puppy. C'mere, puppy. Do you need a new home?"

Ducking his head and shambling forward like he was shy, Cole threw a punch as soon as he was close enough to reach Callum's shoulder. The blow sent him staggering back a step with a laugh, until he bounced against Nolan. Nolan turned too late and toppled into Hudson. The plate of food in Hudson's hands fell to the ground, and a growl filled the air.

"Fuck you. No," Hudson snarled, but it was too late on both their parts.

Fur slid down Hudson and Nolan's arms, and their bears ripped out of their skins. Roars filled the clearing and the two beasts slammed into each other.

"What the fuck is Nolan's problem?"

"Becca. What else? She went drinking with Hud last night." Callum wiped a hand down his face and waded into the brawl, shouting for them to change back and threatening to not set any broken bones before their shift. Cole crossed his arms over his chest and watched the battle rage on. Fuck, did he miss them.

Leah sidled up next to him and he flicked a glance at the woman that'd quickly become like a sister to him. "You look like shit."

She threw an elbow into his side without changing her expression. "You do, too. When do we get to meet her?"

Cole thought of playing innocent and asking who she meant, but there was no chance Leah would believe him. "You? Never. You're a bad influence."

"Sucks for you. That was just a test." Leah shrugged and made a show of picking at her nails. "Guess your lady doesn't share everything with you because Callum and I have appointments this afternoon."

"She's not my lady," he denied automatically. Humans weren't made for enclave life. Humans couldn't be trusted to stay.

Leah was the sole exception. She was cool. She didn't water down the drinks she poured at The Roost, and she'd taught him how to break out of handcuffs. Judah was in for a surprise the next time he tried to drag Cole to the drunk tank.

Then again, Leah was a shifter now. Rylee was still human and still very much working for the government. How much the shadowy organizations and factions within such a beast knew, he had no idea. Rylee certainly didn't know much more than she delightedly rambled on about. She smelled too sweet and innocent and curious when she started talking about the enclave.

But still, he couldn't trust her. She was the epitome of human. Small, weak, fragile. He could hurt her with his pinky and break her with one hand.

His bear rumbled in his head, finally rousing for the day. The thought of hurting Rylee, or letting her feel pain from anyone, had the bear up and ready to attack. Him, or anyone that laid a hand on the small woman, it didn't matter. His bear wanted blood for the threat to their mate.

Cole laced his hands behind his neck and growled a warning when the brawling bears staggered too close. He could easily step in and help Callum pull them apart. Fuck, it'd probably calm him if he waded in and laid into Nolan and Hudson with claws and fangs. Might distract his stupid beast for a time.

Rylee was not his mate. Could not be his mate.

Too human, too smart, too good. He'd corrupt that sweet innocence and ruin her.

And he hated that it sounded like a good idea.

COLE TUGGED OPEN the door to the clinic and prepared to give Rylee an earful for giving him orders. He couldn't protect her if she left his side. And truthfully, he liked being the one to greet her in the morning and hold open the door to his truck for her to climb inside.

As usual, there was hardly anyone in the waiting room. A mother and her son sat in a corner, both smelling anxious. The boy cradled his arm, no doubt broken. The doctor rarely treated anything else.

He swung through the doors to the back after a quick nod of sympathy to the kid, only to find Mayor Olivia Gale blocking his path down the hall and to Rylee's lab. She snagged a handful of his shirt and dragged him into the nearest exam room, shutting the door behind them.

He raised his hands and cracked a smile to combat her scowl. "Easy, Mayor. I'm flattered, but I'm not really looking for anything serious right now."

"You're not looking for anything serious at all, from what I gather. What happened yesterday and why am I hearing about it from that Delano character?" Olivia demanded.

Cole tried to keep his face neutral at the man's name. "I escorted the scientist to the borders, as commanded. Delano's patrol found us and demanded she give him access to her bag. She didn't want to hand it over, he made some threats, and I stepped in."

"You stepped in. That's what you're calling it? I put you on this assignment to keep you and Delano from each other's throats, not to keep pecking at each other. You are to remain silent while watching and learning. Have you done that? No. I don't care how her people treat her. I care about what it means for our people."

His bear roared in his head and Cole saw red. He understood Olivia's reasoning. Putting Bearden first, giving them the opportunity to defend themselves, that sounded good on paper. But when the reality meant letting men like Delano behave like animals, he couldn't agree. And it had nothing to do with the growling, furious beast in his middle demanding to protect Rylee.

The defense sounded weak even in his head.

But the objection still stood. It was only a matter of time before Delano planted his boot on the throats of everyone in Bearden. His treatment of Rylee was a sure indication of that.

"I have a job to get to," he growled. And a not-mate to check on before his bear rattled his way out of his skin. "Did you forget that? The one where you took me away from the firehouse to watch some government nerd get hassled by the military men sitting on our borders?"

Olivia tilted her head and watched him for several long moments. "I have heard nothing from you since Ms. Garland has entered Bearden."

Cole shoved his hands deep into his pockets to keep from throttling her. Callum wouldn't like that, mostly because his brother would have to sit behind a desk until they could find another replacement. And if Callum shifted jobs again, that would mean he'd have to take over in the firehouse. At least he'd be back where he belonged.

"I'm watching her. I don't know what else you want from me. She's talking to people, she's taking samples. She's acting exactly how you'd expect a scientist to act."

Olivia didn't change her expression in the slightest. "I want a report on my desk by the end of the day detailing what has been said in these interviews, who attended, and what she has collected from them. You do know how to write, don't you?"

"Anything else? Should I raise the dead and turn back time so we were never revealed? Or maybe just figure out how to open the damn veil so we can all slip through to the other side?" Cole snapped. He tried to step aside, but Olivia planted a hand on his chest and craned her neck to meet his eyes in a challenge. Small though she was, and certainly not his alpha, the predatory look of her narrowed, black eyes gave him pause.

"Push me, bear. I'll keep you from your firehouse for the rest of your life. I don't care how you do it, but I want to know everything the military and government know about us. Seduce her, hack her, find out everything inside that pretty little head of hers or forget about picking up a hose again. I can't protect Bearden if I don't know the threats we face." Dismissing him entirely, Olivia exited the room and left him behind.

Cole shoved his hands into his hair and tightened his fists. By the Broken, he was going to shatter before long. He was pulled away from his clan and pushed in the path of a woman that could destroy his life. There was no peace in sight. He was spiraling out of control, and the one woman that seemed to slow his fall was exactly the woman he needed to keep away.

Humans weren't meant for enclave life. And Rylee Garland was the most fragile of them all.

CHAPTER 9

Rylee folded her hands in front of her keyboard and tried not to cry. She bit down on her tongue to keep from screaming.

Peter sat next to her direct superior, Foster Ravel.

It'd been years since she'd needed to interact with him, and weeks since the sight of him sent her fleeing her lab to the small town of mysterious Bearden. It appeared he'd taken the job in Nevada after all and ranked higher than her.

He sat there, pleasant expression on his face like he had no crimes in his past. He acted like an innocent man when the reality was he'd stripped her down and taken everything from her.

"I believe you two know each other," Foster said with an air of dismissal. He probably wanted to get back to whatever he was tinkering with. The sooner the better. "Peter will be taking over as head of a team here. I wanted him to sit in and see what we're working on."

Peter smiled widely. "We do. We were in the same doctorate program."

Her ears buzzed like someone turned on a television in a different room. It took all her concentration to nod once to confirm Peter's words.

"Let's get down to it, then," Foster said. "We've received disturbing news from the field officer outside of the Bearden enclave. He said you were in a scuffle with one of the shifter residents and put his men in danger."

Rylee's mouth dropped open. The flash of anger made her temporarily forget her Peter-induced panic. She felt attacked on all sides. There was no peace in the lab back home, nor any to be found with Delano sticking his nose where it didn't belong. "Sir, that's not what happened. I was gathering data with my guide around the enclave, results that have already been forward over to you, when Delano interfered and demanded access to my findings as well as a quick end to the study."

Foster consulted with something on his phone and typed in a quick message. She was used to him working on multiple projects at once. She wasn't used to receiving a disapproving frown. "While you are not under Major Delano's command, we would rather you listen to him. He's on the ground and knows what he's doing to keep you and his men safe. If you aren't able to cooperate with him, then I'll be forced to replace you with someone who can."

"Respectfully, sir, Major Delano isn't doing my work any favors. The people here have been nothing but polite. They're just normal people living out their lives. Delano's insistence on finding them a threat is the chief issue. If the people of Bearden can't trust me because of him, then no one you send here will get any further."

"Normal lives are a bit out of the question, don't you think?" Peter asked condescendingly. "They're hardly human, either."

Rylee flicked her eyes a fraction of an inch to show she acknowledged his words, then focused again on Foster. She couldn't let Peter get under her skin. She couldn't let him take something else from her.

And he was so, terribly wrong. She thought back to her trip to the coffee shop just that morning. Small town mechanics and meddling mother-in-laws were in full swing. There were nerves over changing the family dynamic by bringing a new life into the mix. How many times were scenes and emotions like those played out across the world? Thousands, daily.

Bearden and its residents were normal people with a little bit extra, in her eyes. She wanted to make the rest of the world see it, too.

"Well, that is what Rylee is there to see," Foster defended lightly. "But I recommend you listen to Delano and take extra precautions. These supernaturals, while potentially average individuals, are capable of great damage."

Peter shook his head and drew his brows together. "I saw what they did to Delano's face. I think they're more than capable. I think they're willing and should be treated as a threat. I vote we end study in the field. Bring a handful of them back here, where they can be contained, and we can determine if they're safe for the rest of society."

"No." Rylee cleared her throat to hide her unexpected shrillness. She couldn't return to a lab that held Peter. He should be the one locked in a cage, not Cole or Becca or Faith. "The best results are the ones where they can be observed in their own environment."

Foster nodded. "I agree. For now. You have

received your warning. Don't cross a line with Delano again, or your access will be revoked."

"And on a personal note, give me a call sometime, Rylee. I'd love to catch up." Peter flashed her a smile that didn't reach his eyes.

Barely containing her tears, she closed out the virtual conference program. Her chest tightened, and she shook. Her stomach roiled unsteadily. Only when she was absolutely certain no connection remained open, did she let go of the first sob.

God, she hated what he did to her. She hated how she reacted to him, years after the fact. She hated that the sound of his voice sent her spiraling back into that night of terror.

He'd been so kind to her in the months leading up to their disastrous relationship. He'd been her first real date, besides the pity group gathering for high school prom. She'd always been so focused on pulling herself up through her own hard work and achievements, that she left the awkwardness of first dates and boyfriends to everyone else. Then Peter came along and disarmed her.

Rylee sucked in a shaky breath and tried to turn away from those dark memories. She couldn't afford to dive into them and relive her weakness and stupidity. She should have known something was off about him, should have seen the red flags popping up every which way she turned. She should have fought harder.

Even knowing she wasn't at fault didn't quiet the internal blame. Peter hadn't been dealt justice, so surely something had gone wrong because of her.

The familiar self-loathing rode in right on the heels of her blame game. She hated the knots Peter still tied her in. Hating herself, hating him, blaming herself, blaming him. There was no winning in the dark, loathsome spiral.

And through it all, sobs continued to wrack her body. She rested her forehead on arms crossed over her desk and let her tears fall.

The door crashed open and Cole stomped inside, face twisted into anger. The expression fell from him immediately after his eyes found her. The stormy grey churned to gold, and a growl leaked out of him.

"What's wrong?" he demanded. "Was the mayor in here?"

She shook her head and tried to wipe away her tears, but he was faster.

He knelt by her side before she could open her mouth and swiped a thumb over her cheeks.

Concern wrinkled his brows. "What happened, then?"

For such a huge man, he could be so gentle. Despite—or maybe because of—the animal he kept packed away inside him, she felt safe. He could tear her apart in an instant, but she doubted he'd ever come close. Anyone who harmed her, maybe. And that didn't sound so horrifying.

A large part of her wanted to see Peter sporting the mark of claws and fangs. She wanted to see all her internal hurt splayed across his skin.

But the other, saner part of her knew it would do no good. A momentary thrill wouldn't heal all the scars she carried.

"You can tell me," he said, mouth twisting like he hated the taste of the words.

Even if his words were sour on his tongue, his hands were soft on her. He held her by the shoulders, thumbs gently circling over her skin. Each pass soothed away some of her panic. His fingers were rougher than she expected. She felt silly for even considering it and disliked his needing to comfort her.

She shook her head and swallowed back her sorrow. "I'm fine," she insisted.

Surprisingly, with him so close, it wasn't far from

the truth. The safety he extended to her soothed the fear that spiked at the sight of Peter. She didn't need to relive her horrors with Cole nearby. "Just work stuff."

He didn't push for more or call her out on her lie. It *was* work related, but not in the way that should send her into a fit. The swirling gold of his eyes didn't fade one bit as he rocked onto his heels and looked at her expectantly. Did he want her assurance again, or was he waiting for her to spill her secrets?

Neither were about to happen. She gave him a tight smile and wiped away the last of the wetness on her cheeks. "I should get some kits ready. Two volunteers are coming in this afternoon."

Cole frowned, concern still lining his face. "I heard. My brother and his mate, Leah. And it's not happening. Not today. Not when you're like this. I'm going to reschedule everything for tomorrow, and you take it easy."

"I shouldn't—"

"You should. Keep the details to yourself if you want, but you look like a raccoon and your heart is beating faster than a hummingbird's. You're not going to get anything if you look, sound, and smell like prey and I couldn't stand to watch anyone chase you."

Rylee ran her tongue over her lips and his eyes dropped to follow the motion. The air around Cole, and extending over her, felt heavy and sounded like more was meant to be said. They shared that, then, telling half-truths. For the first time in a long while, she wanted to tell someone everything.

She took a few deep breaths and imagined locking Peter behind a dark wall in the back of her mind. Everything that came with him, all the fear and shame and panic, went in with him. Then she closed the solid door and walked away.

Keeping that part of her locked down was necessary. She had a job to do, and she needed to prove the Major Delanos and Peters of the world wrong. The supernaturals weren't any more a threat than some random person on the street.

And to know the other half of the words Cole left hanging in the air, she couldn't let the past drag her down. "Thank you," she said.

CHAPTER 10

Rylee peeked around the door of her samples fridge when she heard the familiar sound of Cole's boots stomping down the hall. She expected him to scold her for again slipping into the lab before he had a chance to pick her up that morning, but he surprised her by launching straight into the day's agenda.

"Callum and Leah are almost here," he said. "They left the cabins right behind me."

She let the fridge door fall closed, then reached for the nearest notepad and pen. She felt calmer with something to focus on. She needed to stay focused; the day would be packed with catching up on the interviews he rescheduled for her.

She'd felt so silly when she shut the door to her

room at Muriel's, but a long bath brought another round of crying and then a strange sort of exhaustion. He'd been right that she wasn't fit to work. The brief bit of contact with Peter sent her down a rabbit hole of emotion she thought she'd been able to tame.

Cole had been sweet to deliver food at lunch and dinner. She hadn't seen him, probably by design, but the messages on her phone to eat and the to-go boxes left outside her door were clear enough that he'd checked up on her throughout the day.

Her grip on the pen tightened. It centered her to the work she needed to do, instead of letting her mouth run wild with thanks and conversation she didn't want or even know how to begin.

She cleared her throat. "Explain that term to me that you used yesterday. Mate. You and one of the girls at the coffee shop both used it."

Cole took his customary seat in the corner. His frown of concern turned into a scowl. The gold of his eyes brightened, but he shifted his gaze away from her. "It's like marriage, but more serious. Life-long, soul mate sort of bullshit. Our animals choose."

"How?" She stopped doodling a heart with only one side complete. Focus, she reminded herself. Cole simply showed her a bit of decency. That wasn't a reason to fall into a crush.

"Smell, for one. Taste, to confirm. Callum says there's this overwhelming need to be near the other person. It's like you can't breathe without them." Cole's grimace deepened. "Ask him. I don't know."

Rylee tapped her pen against the notepad. "And everyone has one?"

He shrugged uncomfortably. "I assume. But not everyone meets one. Some, most maybe, just settle down with someone compatible."

She glanced up, then back down to her notes. Her palms itched and her stomach turned over, but not with the queasy disgust she felt earlier.

Butterflies. That's what she felt. Wanting to know if Cole had someone in his life made her feel butterflies in her stomach.

"And do you have a mate?" she asked softly.

"No," he said forcefully. "I don't want one."

"He doesn't know what he's talking about. Mates are wonderful," a woman said from the door.

Rylee smiled at the couple entering her lab. She could see the resemblance between the men. Both were massive with wide shoulders and huge arms. Callum was carved from rough stone, but Cole was made with a more delicate hand. He hid the difference under his tattoos and a thicker bit of stubble on his cheeks than his brother carried.

Callum stuck his hand out, but Cole was suddenly between them. "This is Rylee. Rylee, this is Callum, my brother and alpha, and Leah, his mate."

"Down, boy." Leah snorted and reached around him to shake Rylee's hand.

Callum shifted his eyes to her, then to his brother. "Better listen to her, Cole. She's on a tear this morning. She might just take second from you."

Rylee cocked her head. "Can you expand on that while I pull the kits? Please, take seats. You don't need to linger in the door."

"Better listen to her, Callum. She's on a tear this morning. She might just take all our secrets from you," Cole teased and wheeled his seat to the table in the middle of the room.

"If you two are done measuring your dicks, I'll answer the lady," Leah announced and flounced into one of the waiting seats. "Alpha is the leader of our little bands of misfits. That's Callum. Second is just that, second in command. Which is Cole, when he's not sciencing the shit out of things."

Rylee spread out a cloth and snapped on gloves. Tubes were ready to hold cheek swabs and hair samples for both Leah and Callum. Needles were ready to draw blood. She gestured to Callum to roll up his sleeve, and she cleaned his skin. "How many are typically grouped together under one leader?"

"Depends on the alpha," Callum answered. She set the needle against the vein as he continued without a wince. "Some are stronger and can hold more. Some are happy with just one person under them. Some are content staying a loner."

"I need a few hairs, root and all. This might sting a little," she warned after putting a sticker on the vial with Callum's blood. The back of her neck prickled with raised hairs. Glancing over her shoulder, she found both Cole and Leah watching her with wary eyes. She felt hunted.

Callum reached up and pulled a few hairs out himself. "Will this do?"

Able to breathe again, she nodded. "Back to mates. Cole said there's a draw to the other person." She flicked a glance at Cole. "Is that only between shifters, or is it felt when someone is fae or vampire?"

"Or human? I felt it with Callum before I was bitten. Not as strongly as a shifter, but there was this pull to him. A need to be near him. Protect him. Defend him from anyone who oversteps," Leah nodded, still watching her closely.

The air felt like jelly as Rylee stuck Callum's hair

into a tube and sealed it shut. She reached for the cheek swabs and quickly rubbed inside Callum's cheek. Her hands shook when she stuffed them into their tube. "No overstepping," she soothed. "Simply doing my job."

Silence reigned as she changed gloves. Leah held out her arm for her sample to be taken. "Have you felt a pull to anyone before?" Leah asked.

Rylee's heart jumped in her chest and she looked again toward Cole. He wasn't interested in a mate. He'd know if he had one, from her crash course on the subject. And while she did feel inexplicably drawn to him, there was no future. She'd finish her work and be done with Bearden.

"No one," she said quietly.

She'd barely pulled the needle from Leah's arm when the woman flattened her hands on the table and squeezed her eyes shut. A rattle worked its way out of her middle, and her eyes were liquid silver when she opened them again. Cole was immediately on his feet, placing himself between them.

"Need to go," Leah growled, inhuman.

"Shit. Yeah. Out the door. Nice meeting you, Rylee," Callum lifted Leah by her shoulders and hustled her out the door. Leah's rumble grew louder even as they hurried through the clinic.

A dull roar hit the air, followed by a tiny, delighted screech of children and clapping of hands.

Rylee turned wide eyes to Cole. "What just happened?"

He made a face and returned to his seat. "What you said the first time we met, about shifters spreading to others unwillingly? Leah was bitten during a challenge fight. No knowledge or consent. It fucks with the animal, no matter how much you would want it. Those people can be dangerous when their animal takes control."

"She was going to change? Here?" She toyed with the collar of her blouse. As much as she wanted to see a shift happen up close, she certainly didn't want it in her lab. Too many things—herself included—could be broken in the tiny space.

Cole twisted in his seat and drew up the back of his shirt. She swallowed hard at the glimpse of the cut muscles wrapping around to his front. On closer inspection, though, she could see faint scars across his side. "She got me last week before Callum could draw her off. He's the only one that can contain her right now. Probably a combination of alpha power and being her mate."

She must have looked horrified, because he dropped his shirt and continued. "Don't worry, little

123

bit. I won't let her hurt you. And fights are normal with us. We have to keep finding our place in the clan, and beating the shit out of one another is one way to work off some steam and keep the pecking order."

Nodding, she mulled over everything that had taken place. There was mobility within the ranks, just as there was within the military or any job. It wasn't based on merit, but a sense of power. She wondered if there was a way of measuring or predicting that, and if it would be expressed through any particular genes.

She settled into routine. She needed to start the sequencing of both samples, since those would take the longest. Then she wanted to start the amplification of some interesting segments of samples previously gathered and sequenced.

But first, she wanted to prep slides and get a quick visual of the blood cells themselves. So far, she'd seen nothing different in the shape or size in any of Bearden's residents that would point to anything similar to sickle cell anemia. The only unusual aspect had been the concentration in the sample taken from the vampire, Victor.

The first slide presented nothing unusual, but the second showed slight variations. The cells weren't twisted into a new shape, but they weren't as round as she was used to seeing. Tiny, gentle ridges made up the outsides.

"Oh. Oh! Come see this!" She didn't even move from the eyepiece, only waving Cole toward her. The roll of his chair sounded loud in the quiet lab and she shifted to the side to make room for him.

Cole pulled back from the eyepiece after barely putting his face to the microscope. "I can't see shit."

"Oh. Sorry." Rylee dropped her glasses from the top of her head to her nose and pressed back against the eyepiece. A quick twist of a knob adjusted the settings for normal sight and she made room for him again. "Try that."

He'd barely ducked his head back to the eyepiece when she started explaining. "See the ridges on one, but not the other? Most of what I've seen so far are smooth, which makes sense if everyone was born a shifter. But Leah was bitten, right, and her cells show a slight difference in structure.

"I'll know more once the sequencing finishes tomorrow, but I bet there will be little differences here and there. Slips in the code, if you will. Not enough to be an entirely different species. Almost like a different breed. Both shifters, just slightly different."

He looked at her like she spoke another language. "And you can tell all that from some blood and hair?"

"Neat, isn't it?" She nodded, enthusiasm seeping into her words. Shyness suddenly fell over her. She wanted him to share in her excitement. A little bit of acceptance, that was all she wanted. By his own words, he wasn't interested in the subject.

"I don't understand half of it, but very neat." He tucked a stray piece of hair behind her ears and then fixed her glasses on her face. The stormy weather in his eyes coalesced into a swirl of gold. "You seem better today."

"Something unexpected came up, is all." Panic and fear and everything that came with thinking about Peter rose hot and disgusting in her throat. She pushed it back down, determined not to let it consume her. She was safe in Bearden. Safe near Cole. Peter wouldn't stand a chance against the man, let alone the beast. "I wanted to thank you for yesterday and I wasn't sure how. You just stepped right in and... and..."

"It was no problem. You were upset. Anyone would have done the same."

Her lips twitched into a sad smile. "No. They wouldn't."

"You've been around the wrong people, then," he

said. His words were quiet, but the air felt heavy again, like it had the day before when he found her crying. She wanted to wrap herself in it like a blanket.

Her breath caught in her chest as he leaned forward. She expected to feel panic and fear, those wild emotions she was most familiar with since Peter's attack.

Cole pressed his lips to hers and a tiny rumble vibrated through him and into her. That sensation delivered heat all over her body, from her tight shoulders all the way to her toes. Her scalp tingled at the second vibrating rumble and she nearly gasped. It was almost like a purr.

She'd been kissed before, even before Peter took advantage, but nothing quite like Cole. He took his time, sipping her lips until he teased her into parting them. The first stroke of his tongue pulled a tiny, shocked groan from her that he devoured with a sexy growl. The rest of the world faded away in the background and it was just them, sharing breath and tasting one another.

He cupped her cheeks, and she expected him to turn rough. Maybe rough wasn't the right word. Less gentle. More demanding. But he kept his slow, deliberate pace. His lips, his kiss set her on fire.

She should have felt panicked. He held her close. He could overpower her at any moment. Where she expected to want to run, she wanted to get closer. That in itself tinged the kiss with a bit of panic. What did it mean that the giant, grumpy shifter could so solidly brush away everything that'd held her back from truly living? There was a hook in her middle that felt connected to him, slowly reeling her closer into his orbit.

She wasn't sure if it was something she was ready to examine.

She sucked down a shuddering breath when he finally let her loose. He didn't part from her, though. He only pressed his forehead to hers and plucked once more at her lips. "I've been chasing the wrong girls all my life if all nerds kiss like that."

Rylee shut her eyes, but that didn't wash away her smile or the flush spreading across her cheeks. "You're ruining it."

He smirked. "Little bit, you don't even know the half of it."

CHAPTER 11

"Morning," Cole greeted Rylee. One shy smile was enough to send his dick thudding against his zipper. He'd had another night filled with dreams of her and been out of bed even before his alarm sounded.

Worryingly, she didn't say a word and huddled near the door. Brows shooting together, he tested the air. She didn't smell nervous or scared, not in the way he'd expect if she regretted what'd happened between them. She smelled almost… apprehensive. Like she was waiting for something bad to happen.

Cole's frown deepened. He pushed her too far. One kiss was too much. She knew as well as he did that they were dangerous together.

That damn kiss had torn his world apart. His

bear, smug bastard, still refused to see the truth of the situation. Rylee might be fun for a night or a month, but she wasn't his future. She was human and humans weren't meant for enclave life. She'd be out of Bearden once her lab had enough results and then she'd go on to start her perfect human family with some shitty human husband. He and the rest of Bearden would be entirely forgotten. He'd seen it before with his own mother.

His jaw tightened, and he didn't try to tease a word out of Rylee. She shifted in her seat next to him, throwing glances his way, but he didn't say a damn word. Her baby blues grew bigger and more watery the longer they went without speaking.

His phone chimed through his truck speakers and he answered the call with a growl. "What?"

"Cole," his father's nurse, Louise, breathed into her phone. "I couldn't reach Callum. It's Ephraim. He's had an episode again."

Cole passed a hand over his face. He did not want to deal with an out of control bear, not when he couldn't even deal with the silent treatment from his unwilling companion. "Can you try him again?" he asked, knowing the answer even before Louise denied him. She wouldn't be calling him if she had a hope of reaching Callum.

"Can you please come?"

Cole growled an acceptance and ended the call. He turned to Rylee. "Need to make a pit stop."

She didn't say a word, only nodded when he turned down a different street than the one they took toward the clinic. A few more turns put them on a potholed road and he saw Louise's car peeking out of the driveway.

Cole pulled up alongside Pop's nurse and rolled down his window. "What happened?"

Louise wrapped her hands around her steering wheel. "It was a normal morning. Served him grapefruit and had coffee. Callum stopped by, as usual. He'd been gone for maybe an hour when Ephraim started acting agitated. I tried to calm him, and then he snapped that he didn't know me, and shifted. That's when I reached for the tranquilizer, but he got me before I could pull it out."

Cole whistled when Louise raised her arm and showed the healing scratches. At least she'd been able to dodge before those scratches turned to full wounds. Blood made his father crazy when he was already in a state. "I'll handle him from here. Thanks, Louise."

He nodded and eased his truck past the nurse. Rylee hadn't said a word before he pulled to a stop in front of his father's house and he cut her off before she could object to anything. "Wait here. I don't want you getting hurt."

"What's going on?"

He was already out of the truck and jogging toward the house. He shouted over his shoulder, "Stay there."

The house was a mess, but not nearly as bad as he expected. Pop had changed in the kitchen. Scraps of clothes littered the floor, and one of the chairs hadn't survived. The door leading to the backyard was just gone, broken into pieces by the sharp claws and heavy paws of a bear determined to break free.

He grabbed the tranq gun from inside a locked drawer, right where Louise said it would be. She'd been able to shove the keys into the lock before Pop chased her off. With that in mind, Cole stuffed a couple extra darts into his pocket, in case the first didn't bring his father down.

He was out the broken back door in an instant. By the fucking Broken, he hated tracking his father like an animal. Pop's scent was strong enough that he didn't need to look hard before he found the aging bear circling around the house and ambling toward his truck.

And Rylee. Fuck. He couldn't let her get hurt. It

didn't matter that Bearden would be blown off the map as soon as a human was injured by someone like him. He, personally, couldn't see Rylee Garland take an injury.

Smug as fuck bear in his middle chuffed in his head until Cole kicked him to the back of his mind. Instincts be damned.

Cole hurried along, gun raised and ready to shoot as soon as he got close enough for the dart to piece through fur and hide. His bear raged inside him, first at the threat to his mate and then at the pain of his father and former alpha falling apart.

Cole shook his head to center himself. He didn't have time for his bear's whining or tantrum. He had to hunt down his father before the man could hurt someone or himself.

He padded silently through the broken brush, keeping the large bear ahead of him. The beast stopped and sniffed the air, but didn't turn. Cole crept closer, then closer still. Finally in range, he squeezed the trigger just as the bear bolted for his truck.

Rylee's scream split the air and dug into his brain. The bear tripped over one of his feet, caught himself, then toppled to the ground right next to the truck.

Slowly, fur receded into skin. Rylee stared at him

from inside the cab, then switched her focus at the first sound of snapping bones. She watched in fascinated horror as the bear changed into his unconscious and naked father.

Blowing out a breath, Cole stooped and lifted his father into his arms. The creaking of his truck door opening and closing didn't give him pause. He walked quickly toward the house and settled his father into his bed. He'd be out for a few hours.

Leaving Pop to sleep, Cole gathered the dustpan and broom from the kitchen pantry and started sweeping shards of glass and smaller bits of wood into a pile. The door would need to be replaced entirely.

"You should head to the lab," he told Rylee as soon as he smelled her behind him.

"Cole," Rylee said softly. She surprised him by reaching for the broom. "I'll clean up the glass if you clear out the wood."

She started at one corner of the kitchen while he piled up broken pieces of door and chair. "What's wrong with him?"

Cole shrugged. "Dementia of some form. He forgets everyone around him and that he has a bear inside him. Makes him dangerous when he shifts or gets forceful. He used to be mayor, and fire chief before that. And now he needs someone watching him every second of the day."

He tightened his jaw and followed a kicked piece of wood out the hole that used to be a door. He needed fresh air. Rylee took up too much inside and he couldn't breathe around her or the memories of how strong his father used to be.

Most of the glass had been swept up by the time he was able to return. He gathered the last few big pieces and leaned against the wall, watching Rylee sweep another pile of glass into the dustpan.

Her brows wrinkled together when she realized he stood there. "How often does this happen?"

His bear roared in his head, unwilling to even think about the sickness ravaging his father. Callum was the good son who forced himself to visit, but Cole had a hard time watching Pop forget him a little more each day. He'd always been in Callum's shadow and accepted his role as spare to Callum's heir. But that didn't make losing a man he admired from afar any easier. "He has an uncontrolled shift about once a week. They're not usually this bad."

"I meant in the population. Look, I know there are more enclaves. What is the rate of cases like this?"

"I don't know. It's not really discussed. We're

supposed to be strong. No illness should touch us. No one likes to admit there's a weakness."

"This is what I could help with. Tracking, researching, comparing to the rates of human population. And maybe linking into what's already been learned from human trials. Prevention and treatment have come a long way."

"But not long enough. There's nothing that will put his mind back together, is there?"

She flinched, and he immediately regretted the sharpness of his words. She was just trying to help. She wasn't the cause of Pop's illness or the lack of treatment available.

Cole stuffed his hands into his hair and blew out a breath. "I'm sorry."

The damage was already done. She retreated into her silence.

Fuck, he was being pulled in too many directions. Callum had his plans and ways of doing things and suggestions about every-fucking-thing. Leah had her own unwanted advice on how everyone in the clan should lead their lives and solve all their problems.

Then there was that horrid Olivia Gale. Mayor Gale had her own demands. And technically, yes, he owed his allegiance to her. She assigned him to watch over Rylee and learn all her secrets. Even when he wanted to keep the tiny woman at a distance, Gale was pushing him closer.

He was caught between a rock and a hard place. His clan alpha wanted him back on fire duty, but that meant listening to the town mayor who held that fate in her hands. He wanted to keep a human woman at a distance, but Olivia wanted him to learn everything Rylee had in her head and her notes.

And then there was Rylee herself. Nervous talker and smarter than he'd ever be, with wicked curves that made him strain against his pants. His bear didn't just push him to get near her; the beast flat out shoved him in her direction. He couldn't even sleep without seeing her face in his dreams.

She couldn't be his mate. Couldn't, shouldn't, wouldn't. She was too human. She'd leave at the drop of a hat. He was too young to remember his own mother's swift departure from Bearden, but he saw what it did to his father. The man stayed strong for his boys, but the wounds were there. And Cole didn't want to be sour and alone once Rylee inevitably left the enclave.

The excuses sounded worn and stale.

CHAPTER 12

Cole tested the new door and set the tools on the kitchen counter to be put away later. He inhaled deeply and let Rylee's scent roll over him. Coating him, more like it. His bear wanted to roll in it.

She hadn't left and was easy to track to the living room. He'd told her to head to the lab while he finished cleaning up, but she hadn't disappeared for more than a second to grab her bag from the truck and then tuck herself into the couch. The silent insistence to stick around made his head swim almost as much as her scent filling his lungs.

He leaned against the wall and crossed his arms over his chest, just drinking her in. She frowned at whatever was on the screen, lips pursing together and hand twisting nothing at her throat. She was beautiful and gorgeous, all the words women liked to hear.

And maybe, for a little while, she could be his. He just couldn't let himself get lost.

"I thought you were heading into the lab."

Rylee looked up from her laptop and a slow smile spread across her face. "I thought I'd stick around in case you needed any help. And maybe if you needed someone to listen."

"Pop will be out for another few hours and we're all cleaned up. I could make us some lunch if you're determined to stick around." The suggestion was out in the open before he had a chance to think about it. And it sounded fucking perfect to his bear. Keeping her safe wasn't the only instinct she triggered. He needed to provide for her. Feed her. He'd kept her flush with food when she had her little breakdown. He could keep her happy and fed again.

She shut her laptop and set it on the side table. "Lunch sounds perfect. What's on the menu?"

Her, if he could manage it.

She padded into the kitchen after him, but he gave no sign that he knew exactly how close she was. Hell, even if he shut his eyes and blocked his ears, he could probably still say the exact distance between them. There was a current that ran from him to her, something vaguely electrical, that he couldn't ignore.

"Sandwiches, probably. We could order something if you want anything fancier than that."

She peeked into the fridge under his arm. Wildflowers and rain entered his nose, all from her. His bear rumbled in his middle, wanting to take control. The beast sent him all sorts of images of Rylee with a mark on her shoulder, proclaiming her off limits to all others. *Mate.*

Not when she'd leave. But fun could be had before then. He could think of her as he thought of every other woman he slept with: temporary.

Convincing his bear that she wasn't anyone important was for later.

He twisted around, catching her around the waist and letting the fridge fall shut. One hand sifted into her hair and the other held her close. Two steps backward pushed her against the wall between kitchen and living room.

He dropped his lips to her neck, relishing in the feel of her riling up his human half and soothing the animal. "I can't stop thinking about you. Wanting you."

Fear entered her scent. The sting of it itched at

his nose and forced him to back off. He pulled away, searching her face for any answers. "What's wrong?"

"I… I can't," she mumbled, not meeting his eyes.

"Is this where you tell me you're not supposed to sleep with anyone in town? You can. We can. We're grown adults and can make our own choices."

"I'm not—that's not..." Another wave of fear wafted off her, growing stronger with every passing second. "Cole, I can't!"

She shoved at his chest and he took a hasty step back from her. She planted one hand against the wall and the other over her heart, pulling breath after breath into her lungs and still not getting enough air.

He cocked his head and tried to understand what went wrong. He thought she'd been more than willing. Hell, she smelled like she wanted him more and more leading up to that kiss that branded his soul. Maybe she was virginally nervous. "Have you ever been with a man?"

"Yes—no. Not in the way you mean," she whispered, big blue eyes tracking him as he stalked around the living room.

"Fuck," he snarled, shoving his hands into his hair and pacing. He made a circuit around the living room and turned, finding her big blue eyes watching him warily.

He needed to stop. He was making her more nervous. His need to burn off energy to keep from punching the walls into oblivion wasn't as important as soothing her.

He took a seat on the couch, arms resting on his thighs and hands stuffed into his hair. He hoped he made himself small enough, but even seated he was still almost eye level. He willed his bear to the back of his mind. No gold eyes, no snarls. He was the epitome of calm for her.

Please, please let him be wrong. He didn't want to believe it. Not her. She was too sweet for someone to hurt her. It had to be something else. Otherwise, he'd kill someone.

Pieces of an uncomfortable puzzle slid into place. She didn't like being surprised, and she was wary near anyone larger than herself, which was over half the fucking population. She forced him as far from her as possible on the first day. All the nerves and fear she displayed suddenly made sense and turned his stomach.

Red swam in his vision and his bear clawed at his middle. Blood. Blood needed to spill for her.

"His name. Give me his name."

"Peter Glasser," she breathed. Her shoulders slumped like a weight had been lifted. Even so, she still spoke to the floor instead of him. "Cole, I'm sorry. I shouldn't have gotten close to you. This is my fault."

He lifted his head and locked his eyes on her. "You can't possibly think I'm upset with you."

Her head snapped up, and she stared at him blankly. Seconds passed, and the gulf of miscommunication seemed to narrow between them. "You're not?"

"Of course not." He shook his head, no doubt mirroring her bewilderment. "I want to kill him. I will kill him, if it's the last thing I do. But I can't be upset with you."

For the first time in a long while, he and his bear were one. He'd track down the bastard that hurt Rylee and make him pay. Lots of slow pain waited for the man.

As for Rylee, she needed to be treated right. All that damage done to make her scared of people needed to be erased. He wanted to show her how a real man treated his woman.

She could leave after that. He could even accept it. But he needed to help her heal. He needed to show her she had nothing to fear from him or whatever human man came after him, as much as that thought made his stomach clench with hatred for the faceless future.

Fuck Olivia and her obsessive need to know what was in store for them. He'd get close to Rylee, on Rylee's terms.

He patted the seat next to him. "Will you come here? My bear is going crazy making you scared and having you all the way over there."

She nodded. Her first step was faltering, but she grew confident by the time she stopped in front of him. She slashed her eyes to the seat next to him, then tightened her jaw and planted one knee on either side of his lap.

"Rylee," he said, voice tight. His bear pushed forward, rumbling loudly in his head. Loud enough and strong enough to change his eyes gold, he knew.

She touched her tongue to her lips. Determination entered her scent, and she didn't back away. "I want you to hold me."

Cole shut his eyes and willed his bear under control. He wrapped his arms loosely around her middle and, immediately, his bear quieted. The fast thumping of her heart seemed to lessen, as well.

But washing away her fear and his anger was a double-edged sword. With her so close, he was lost in her scent. Wildflowers blossomed all around him, growing thicker with every second. The feel of her straddling him sent the blood rushing straight to his cock, and he was harder than ever in his life.

He refused to move and ease the ache in his jeans. The metal teeth of his zipper could leave permanent indentations and he still wouldn't give in to the urge to thrust his hips against her. He wouldn't set her back. He wouldn't be the cause of her fear. She asked him to hold her, and that was all he would do.

She relaxed into him slowly. Melted against him. A small shift of her hips dragged her against his hard length and she froze. Her breath caught in her lungs, and then she moved again, stroking up and down his shaft.

"You need to stop that, little bit," he groaned. "I want to show you how you should be touched, but you're not ready."

"I'm so tired of him hanging over everything I do."

Cole pulled her back and peered up at her. Rylee shifted again, and he shut his eyes against the pleasure.

"You make me feel brave."

"Brave isn't enough," he denied. Fuck, but he

wanted to bury himself inside her. Fingers, tongue, cock, anything. He wanted to show her how a man should treat a woman.

"Safe, then. Wanted." She swallowed. Her fingers shook when they found the first button of her blouse. "Normal."

"Rylee." A second button came undone and he couldn't tear his eyes away from that bit of skin peeking through the slash. He tightened his grip on her thighs but didn't make any other moves.

"I don't want to be scared for the rest of my life." She worked her fingers down her shirt until the flimsy fabric parted. She shrugged out of it, blonde hair swishing as she twisted to drop it to the floor.

Cole moved then, hands sliding up her back and tangling into her hair. He inhaled a long line up the column of her neck and savored the thickly sweet scent of her. He wanted her badly. Wanted to savor her. Convince her to part for him.

His bear watched eagerly. Quiet, for once. Patient.

Under it all, her heart fluttered too quickly to be just from her arousal. She wasn't ready for everything. Hell, he wasn't entirely convinced she was ready for this.

That thought sent a flash of fury through him and tempered his own desire. She wanted to test her boundaries, see what she could or couldn't manage. She'd deemed him safe enough for that, and he wouldn't disappoint her. He'd rather die than see her eyes go dead and a frown mar her lips.

"I want to kiss you," he murmured below her ear. Another swallow, another nod. Another needle of desire he couldn't acknowledge, pushing him to touch her and claim every inch of her.

"Kiss me."

RYLEE DIDN'T KNOW how long they stayed locked together. Her hands balled into Cole's shirt or stroked down his chest while he stayed the perfect, sexy gentleman. Well, maybe not perfect. There were a few choked groans and hitches of his hips that sent a thrill spilling through her veins, but that was all and seemed almost involuntary. And they excited her more, so she couldn't blame him.

He trailed a line of soft, wet kisses down her neck and over the mounds of her breasts. His hand cupped one while his mouth found the other, sucking her nipple through the cotton. "Perfect. Just fucking perfect," he said thickly, switching places and paying the same amount of attention to her other nipple.

Rylee bit down on her lip to keep from crying out. She didn't have time for fear or panic when Cole was making her drunk on lust. She'd never felt so good. He was leading her back to the land of the living with one pleasurable twist of his mouth at a time.

He released her nipple and gave her another long, lingering kiss that sparked need inside her. His hands moved up and down her legs, along her back, across her stomach. His fingers settled on the button of her slacks. "Can I peel you out of these?"

"I don't know, can you?" Rylee shot back without thinking. She slammed her hands over her mouth in embarrassment.

Cole snorted a laugh. "May I? I didn't know we were in grammar class. Nerd."

Pressing her lips together and ignoring the flutter of fear that wanted to come to life, she nodded. Cole held her eyes as he popped the button, then pulled down her zipper. Gold churned in the grey, fascinating her into relaxing a fraction. Silently, she went to her feet and let him drag her pants down her body.

Then she was nearly naked with another person for the first time in years. Her fingers itched to cover herself until Cole raked his eyes up and down her body. A flush worked its way across her cheeks and down her neck and dropped heat straight to her core.

"You smell so fucking amazing it makes my mouth water. I want to touch you, little bit. Do you know what that means?"

Unable to find her tongue, she nodded.

Cole shut his eyes and inhaled sharply. His hands tightened around her thighs, but he didn't move. "Need to hear you say yes," he said, voice thick and low.

"Yes," she breathed.

He pulled her into his lap again, lapping and sucking at her nipples while one hand, one impossibly hot hand, slipped beneath the lace of her panties.

Rylee gasped when his finger slid through her curls. He circled her entrance slowly, giving her every chance to take back her agreement. The words were there on her tongue, ready to push him away, until they suddenly died.

She didn't want to give into old panic. She wanted to see what Cole could give her.

He slid one finger deep inside her and drew a ragged moan from her lungs. Just that threatened to send her flying into the unfamiliar. That touch alone erased the last bit of fear lingering in her veins. She wanted more.

Cole was there to provide. He added a second finger to the first, and she stretched deliciously around him. Her sudden intake of breath jerked his head up and he fixed his eyes on hers.

He stared straight into her very being as he pumped his hand against her.

Rylee wanted to shut her eyes, wanted to lose herself to the darkness behind her lids, but she couldn't. She met Cole's gaze with naked longing. There was a promise in his eyes, convincing her that he meant her no harm. He lived for her pleasure.

Each thrust of his fingers bumped and curled against her sweetest spot and drew pants from her lungs. He played her body like an instrument he'd mastered and cherished for years. Her hips bucked against him, taking his touch, loving how he felt inside her, daring him to look away.

Then she shattered amid his throat growls and her panted, mewling moans.

Still locked with his eyes and gasping for breath, Rylee rode the thick waves of pleasure that pulsed through her. The spasms intensified until she had to shut her eyes, had to just let herself *feel* what she'd never attained on her own, and rarely wanted to try after... after...

Cole didn't slow and ripped another orgasm out of her right on the heels of the first.

It was his deep growl that forced her eyes open again. Her stomach hollowed with every gulped breath, and a new flush of excitement zinged through her when he stuffed his fingers in his mouth and licked them clean.

"You taste as good as you smell," he told her with a smirk on his lips.

Her hands fluttered at her sides and her mouth worked wordlessly. She had no fathomable idea of what to say to that and she fell back to her idea of what normal looked like. She should reciprocate in some way. "What about you?"

He ducked his head and kissed her neck. "I'm fine. Don't worry about me."

"That doesn't seem fair."

He dragged her hand to his crotch and over the thick outline of his cock. He twitched under her fingers but still pulled her hand higher and closer to the waist of his jeans. Her fingertips touched warmth and understanding flooded through her.

His voice was thick when he spoke and his eyes swirled with a brighter gold. "That's how much I enjoyed getting you off. And when you're sure, absolutely sure, we can do more."

It was a promise she aimed for him to keep.

CHAPTER 13

Settled into her rented room for the night, Rylee checked her email for one last round of messages before she turned off the lights and went to bed. Her eyes and limbs felt heavy enough that she didn't think she'd had trouble falling, or staying, asleep.

She fingered her lips, imagining she could still taste Cole. Her stomach tightened with the flood of memory from that afternoon. He'd touched her and dumped pleasure into her system with barely a trace of panic.

He soothed her. Somehow, someway, he turned off all the responses that kept her actively away from people. He made her feel whole. It was something she'd cherish for always and tempted her to try more.

She bit back a tiny moan as she imagined his fingers sliding into her heat. That image faded and revolved into something else entirely. Hard everywhere, he parted her and sent fire through her with one single stroke.

When she was ready, he said. She could have more of him when she was ready.

She wondered what he'd look like naked. She hadn't seen him shift, which she knew involved the shedding or shredding of clothes. The dark tattoos on his arms spread up under his shirt and she wanted to see just how far and how dark they all were.

He claimed a part of her heart that afternoon. Asking and never pushing, he gave her space when she didn't know she needed it. He didn't try to take more from her, even when her own brain tricked her into thinking she wanted everything he had to offer. It was a tease, sure, but one she needed. Alone in her room and away from the sense of him nearby, she knew it'd been the right decision on his part.

She wasn't ready to sleep with him. Yet. But she could be. It was no longer an impossibility. He'd pushed her broken pieces back into roughly the shape she'd been before. It was up to her to glue them together.

Absently, Rylee clicked on a notification of new files shared onto the remote hard drive used between her and the lab in Nevada.

The documents started out innocuously enough. Policy and procedure, mostly. Things she'd seen before in lab settings throughout her college years, then more when she was recruited to work on for top security projects. Who to report to, what should be reported, how those reports should be formatted.

She kept reading.

There was an epidemic model showing the spread of the shifter contagion that grossly exaggerated the possibility, even if Cole hadn't assured her that shifters didn't regularly bite non-shifters.

Her initial findings on the difference in blood cells between bitten shifters and humans, as well as the concentration of cells in vampiric individuals, were also included as a potential detection measure to distribute to health care providers and emergency rooms.

Then she found one that made her stomach turn. She shot out of bed and dug through her bag until she found a USB stick. Stuffing it into the port, she quickly copied everything to her own drive.

Good thing, too. As soon as the copy finished, her access refreshed, and the files disappeared.

Rylee twisted her fingers and stared in horror at the words on her screen. She was looking at documents outlining the eradication of Bearden's supernatural residents.

The plan called for legitimate provocation before any action was taken, and required clearance through channels higher than the field officer on the ground.

Once provocation was determined, evacuations of nonessential personnel and civilians would be necessary. A large contingent of uncooperative citizens needed removal before any operation could succeed. Controlled fires were suggested, as well as the leaking of a severe threat from an enclave citizen or citizens to the media. Stories originating from the local media were preferred for an air of legitimacy. A list of active reporters in the towns surrounding Bearden followed.

When the civilian element ceased to be a problem, the military camp would dive into their duty by securing and cutting off water and power, including the jamming of wireless signals. Any personnel with the ability to see through the barrier hiding the town would be used to ferry others into the enclave, where they would then surround and shut down any resistance.

Phone in hand, she considered her options. She could call Cole or Bearden's mayor and let them have everything. They could get the story out first and prepare to defend themselves.

Or... she could dig deeper. The government was notorious for considering all options and angles. There were binders full of how to act in case of an invasion from aliens in space or mole people from the core of the planet. The documents accidentally shared with her could be just another case of over preparedness for an eventuality that would never happen.

She didn't want to spark more trouble between the enclave and the military camp on the borders. Telling anyone inside Bearden would do just that. There was already enough suspicion and animosity on both sides without throwing fuel on the fire.

Except Major Delano wanted her to finish her science project so he and his men could get on with their jobs.

Her stomach turned again, and she froze. She didn't know enough to proceed in either direction. She didn't know who she could trust inside Bearden or in her home lab.

She scrolled through her contacts and dialed the number for the sister lab that held the physicists interested in the Broken. The sleeping figures that maintained the magical barrier around the enclave presented a new challenge for their understanding of energy and its capabilities. That alone would have them screaming for more information, but there was also the story of how the ancestors of the supernatural broke through the veil between worlds.

That a geneticist had been invited into the enclave over a physicist still chapped their hides. They hid it well when they spoke to her, though, simply because they couldn't do without more information.

One of them would be perfect for her to feel out for any ominous currents without shuttling her questions up the food chain.

Their main line picked up by one of the underlings who, like herself, was probably doing a final pass of messages and work for the day before heading home.

"Hi, Darcy," she greeted. "Rylee on the ground in

Bearden. I just wanted to check if you had any questions on the last load of docs sent to you."

She'd eaten quiet lunches with the woman before and maintained a pleasant politeness. If there was anyone she considered a friend, it was Darcy.

"Rylee! Good to hear from you! We just finished analyzing the last interviews and measurements. You should see a list of follow-ups tomorrow morning after our group session."

Her shoulders slumped in relief. If the other team was planning to throw more questions and instructions at her, then there wasn't an immediate plan to evacuate nonessentials and civilians from the area. Her own paranoia sparked by seeing Peter and Delano's continued obstinance was making threats out of shadows.

"Thanks for the heads up. Give me a shout if anything changes," she said.

"You know, you can always tag one of us in. You don't have to take everything on yourself. I'd be happy to get out of Nevada for a spell." Darcy tapped something on her keyboard. "Oh! Have you met the new lab lead? Peter? I hear he's angling to get there, too."

Rylee's mouth twisted at his name and the possibility of coming face to face with him. She worked hard to keep emotion out of her voice. "Yeah. We were in the same program."

"Isn't he just so nice?" Darcy gushed in a whisper. "He said he wants to take me out to dinner once he gets settled."

Rylee felt like she'd been punched in the face. Peter had been nice when he started courting her. She thought he'd been perfect. She'd been utterly wrong. "Just... be careful around him. Woman to woman, he's not as charming as he presents himself to be. He really doesn't treat others like they're people. Just objects."

There. Done and warned. She navigated the waters of slander with some office gossip and hoped it'd be enough.

"Oh," Darcy said. Rylee could almost hear her making a face. "That's disappointing. Guess it's back to the jerks and the intimidated online. It's a curse being brilliant and attractive, huh?"

Despite herself, Rylee chuckled. "Yeah. It's a curse."

"What about you? I've looked at some of the pictures you've uploaded for us. Is every single guy there amazing looking? Are you *sure* you can't use an extra hand?"

Rylee smiled into the phone. "You know what,

Darcy, I'll see what I can do. Maybe we can get an extra invitation for you. But until then, you'll just have to forward me what you want done."

There was no chance she was leaving Bearden willingly.

CHAPTER 14

Cole eyed the clock on his truck's dash and then continued scrolling through some search results on his phone. It wasn't quite time to pick up Rylee, and he wasn't going to make her hustle on account of him unable to sit still for a moment longer.

Peter Glasser was a common enough name that he had trouble narrowing down suspects. He pulled Rylee's university name from her career profile and used that as one basis of his search. He didn't even know if that was a lead to follow, but it was a start. She hadn't given him any details, and he wasn't about to push her for more.

But if he ever came across the man, ever knew

for certain he had the right one, he'd make him pay for what had been done to Rylee.

Cole glanced at the clock again and groaned when he saw only a minute had passed. Five more still to go.

Rylee had him acting like some anxious teenager all fucking week. Granted, she made him blow his load like one, too.

And like a teenager, he was biding his time. That's how he chose to frame whatever had sparked between them. His first girlfriend didn't jump right into his bed. Rylee needed soft kisses and coaxing touches. He needed to court her until she was ready.

Cole shut the mental door on his bear before the creature could stick his smug snout into his thoughts. He had enough of images of Rylee with a mate mark on her shoulder. It was never going to happen, no matter how good and perfect she smelled. She wasn't his mate.

He'd let her talk him into working on the weekend on the condition it be a half day only, and she let him take her out to dinner. The last was a promise he wrangled out of her in a supply closet with his back firmly against the wall and her nearest to the door. Even though he gave her the chance to escape, she'd stayed and let him kiss her until her lips were swollen and sexy as fuck.

Finally, the clock ticked over to the exact minute he'd been waiting to arrive and he jumped out of his truck. He picked a flower on the walk up to the front door of Muriel's Bed and Breakfast and ignored the innkeeper's glare as he sauntered right past the desk. He'd made the same journey multiple times since Rylee arrived in Bearden.

Twirling the flower between his fingers, he rapped on the door and waited. And waited. There was a frustrated sound on the other side of the door, then Rylee flung it open.

She'd ditched the professional uniform of blouse and slacks for a plain t-shirt and jeans that hugged her thighs. Her hips were too wide and her top too small to be a runway model, and she didn't move with the grace of someone with an animal in their middle, but damn did she make his bear sit up and take notice.

She twisted her hands at her sides, adjusted her glasses, then stuffed her fingers in her back pockets. "I'm not underdressed, am I? I can go change."

Fuck Peter fucking Glasser for filling her with doubt and uncertainty.

"You're perfect." He stuck the flower behind her

ear, taking notice of the way her breath hitched and a slow, nervous smile spread across her face. She didn't know how to accept compliments. He was going to change that. "Ready?"

"Where are we going?"

"I'm showing you the realest Bearden you'll meet. We're heading exactly three blocks over from the main strip."

"Real Bearden. As opposed to the tourist trap of a handful of shops for all the enclaves that don't exist?" She stiffened slightly and relaxed when he hooked her arm around his elbow and led her out of the inn. "I like the small town charm here. Everything is so close together and everyone seems friendly. Definitely not like where I grew up."

"Where's that?" Cole shut her inside the truck and jogged to his side.

"Tampa. Way too big and sprawling to get anywhere without driving or taking the bus. We lived in a mega apartment complex, one of those huge buildings with ten copies all crowded next to one another. Everyone kept their head down and to themselves. It's just you and your brother, isn't it?"

He blinked at the whiplash of subject. "And our dad."

"I'm the oldest of four. Three girls, one baby boy. I used to want a big family like that."

Cole threw his truck into park on the street next to Hogshead Joint and reached over to squeeze Rylee's thigh. She sounded too sad, and he knew what words she mentally tacked on to her sentence. Before Peter. She'd disappeared into herself after, and he was only seeing flickers of the girl she'd been. It made him want to kill the man even more.

"There's still time," he reassured her. His idiotic bear fed him images of her with a round belly, and Cole clamped down before the beast could force more impossibilities on him. Tiny babies with black or blonde hair wouldn't exist because Rylee wasn't his mate, and she'd leave Bearden behind.

"Maybe," she said politely, but she smelled of utter rejection. Before he could tell her not to lose hope, she opened the door and dropped primly to the ground. "It smells so good."

"Just wait till you taste." Cole took a wide step and adjusted himself. Either he hadn't kept the growl out of his voice, or she was thinking about him as much as he did her, because her cheeks tinged red and wildflowers blossomed in his nose.

He followed her up the stairs to the deck, then directed her to a seat in the corner. Fairy lights wrapped around the railing and extended into the nearest trees. With the parking lot on the opposite side of the building, they had an unobstructed view of the river.

The doors were thrown open, and a number of folks flowed in and out of the building. The servers dodged the patrons and delivered huge plates of food to the shifters in human form. A few bears lingered on the edge of the deck, either relaxing in their animal forms or waiting for others to be done socializing and go for a run.

Tommy's Diner and Mug Shot Coffee Bar were great places, but it was Hogshead Joint that he always craved. There was no room to spread out in town, but the barbecue restaurant was where he could relax. It was designed with shifters in mind: wide aisles indoors and out gave space for any changes, and the deck opened right onto bare earth for those needing a quick getaway on four legs.

He snagged spare menus left on the next table over and flagged down a server when they were ready to order. He was pleased to see that Rylee didn't go straight for the salad, opting instead for a pulled pork sandwich and deliciously unhealthy sides.

Meanwhile, Rylee chatted on about her childhood. School, school, and more school, with the occasional, special trip to science camp. Which he didn't believe existed until she pulled up the website on her phone. And then he couldn't believe anyone would want to go, which prompted her to kick him under the table. He retaliated by snatching a hushpuppy off her plate and stuffing it into his mouth.

She was determined from a very young age. He applauded that drive, but it also made him feel a little sorry for her. While he was running wild in his teens, she was responsibly calculating her GPA. When he briefly left Bearden to try finding his place in the world and made a disastrous discovery, she was years deep into her first degree. He didn't think she'd ever let her hair down and just simply *existed* without some goal in mind.

"There's the mayor." Rylee's words interrupted his thoughts. She paused and tapped a finger against her lips. "You know, the way she made it sound when we first spoke, I expected to actually need a bodyguard. But that hasn't been the case."

Cole shifted in his seat to catch sight of Olivia making a round of the restaurant, no doubt familiarizing herself with Bearden's residents. "You're protected."

"What does that mean? Do I need a bodyguard?" She narrowed her eyes suspiciously.

"It means you're protected. No one will raise a hand against you. It doesn't mean you aren't under threat, though." He twisted around and found all the eyes watching them. "Look closer. The corner to your right, see that group there? Trent leads a bachelor pride of lions. He's had a problem with humans since he watched his parents get poached."

And fuck Trent in particular. He'd gone after Leah while she was still human, and then twice more after she'd gotten her bear. The woman wasn't about to be sliced up by a lion, though. She'd tossed him out of the bar by his mane.

Rylee didn't have that sort of protection. In fact, he feared anyone giving her a dirty look would send her sliding into a panic attack. So he used the same playbook he and Callum came up with when Leah was introduced to Bearden: show the human around on the arm of a shifter, declare her protected, and follow up if anyone stepped out of line.

Only, he was enjoying having her on his arm far too much. And the way Olivia's eyes bored into him, she knew it, too.

"Doctor Garland, what a pleasure to see you out

on the town," Olivia greeted politely when she oh so casually stopped by their table.

Rylee dabbed at the nonexistent sauce on her lips. "Cole's idea. He said if I wanted to observe the real side of Bearden, this is the place to go."

"He's a surprisingly intuitive one, isn't he? How is your research going?"

"Fantastic! I had some promising results on the genetics front, though the physicists are still clamoring for more access with your Broken. If you have time, I'd like to schedule a meeting sometime next week? There's a woman on that team that I think would be a great person to invite into the enclave."

"Give my assistant Allison a call to set something up." Olivia nodded, eyes flicking to Cole. "If you'll forgive me, I need to steal Cole away for a moment. It was very nice chatting with you."

Rylee smiled broadly. "Thank you. And I don't mind at all."

Mood souring, Cole rose to his feet and followed Olivia a short distance away out of earshot of the human.

"What are you doing, Strathorn?" Olivia hissed, keeping her voice low to hide from other shifters.

Cole spread his hands wide. "You wanted me to get closer to her, so that's what I'm doing. You don't get to ride in here on your high horse and tell me that's wrong."

"It looks a little more intimate than that."

His insolence dropped into a growl. "What I do in my bed is no concern of yours. Don't worry, Mayor. She's human and I'm well aware of the danger that brings."

None of the words were lies, but they didn't tell the whole story. He knew humans didn't stick around. He knew what Olivia wanted from him. But he couldn't bring himself to use that bit of intimacy against Rylee. She trusted him for whatever reason and he couldn't betray that. He could puff out his chest and play the lady killer for everyone who watched, but it was all for show.

His bear rumbled a warning to Olivia when she placed her hand on his chest to stop him from heading back to his booth and his woman.

"Watch yourself, Strathorn. Your brother can't protect you forever."

"With all due respect, ma'am, I haven't needed my brother to protect me in years." He plucked her hand from his chest and resisted the urge to scrub off the memory of her touch. "I don't know why you're so obsessed with her. She's one of the good guys. If there was anything wrong, she'd tell us. This woman lives for her beakers and samples and shit. She's not playing a game with us. You, though... Well, if you're determined to make Bearden into your version of a spy thriller, I'm out."

He looked past Olivia and found Rylee glancing around as casually as possible to avoid outright staring. There were more than a few bears on the outskirts of the deck, and the tables and chairs were packed with clumps of people together as a clan or on dates.

"It's not just her we need to worry about. Don't forget who she works for," Olivia answered sharply.

Olivia pushed him to dig out Rylee's secrets and he couldn't. He wouldn't. She owned them and he wouldn't rip them away from her. She'd been shouted at and talked down to by her own people and Olivia was pulling the same crap with him. Fuck 'em all.

Rylee tore at his heart and he knew he was going to get burned. But right then, he didn't give a shit. He just wanted to get back to her. They could find a little comfort in each other before everything blew up in their faces.

COLE WAS a thundercloud as he stormed back to their table. Rylee stilled. Whatever had happened when Mayor Gale pulled him aside, it hadn't been good.

"You want to get out of here?" Cole asked, barely sitting on the edge of his seat. His fingers drummed against the table and he shot angry glances to anyone who dared look their way.

"I'm finished," she said quietly and pushed her plate away.

A wince passed across his face and he pressed his hands flat. Agitation still clung to him like a second skin, but he was holding it back from her. "Sorry. It's not you. Finish eating if you're not done."

She shook her head. "It's fine, really." She popped one last hushpuppy between her lips. It really was delicious, but she couldn't taste anything at that moment. Cole was upset about something and it spilled over to her. "All done."

He stood, shoving his chair back as he moved, and threw a handful of bills onto the table. "Let's go," he growled. "I don't want to stay here a moment longer than necessary."

Silently, she nodded. She expected him to take her back down the stairs and to his truck, but he led her through the restaurant and out the front door.

She dug in her heels and pulled them to a stop on the edge of the sidewalk.

His agitation and the unknown location swirled a hint of fear in her. The night had gone so well right up to his aside with Mayor Gale. She wasn't about to let worry get the best of her. "Where are we going?"

Cole glanced down at her and another dose of tension sloughed off him. He favored her with a smile that dared her to trust him. "You wanted to see all of us, didn't you? See how clans work together?" She nodded, and he stepped off the sidewalk and into the street. "The Strathorns are hitting up the bar tonight and I could use a drink."

Feeling unsure, but desperate to give a night out with Cole a shot, she hurried after him. He held the door open and a wave of country music washed over her. Laughter and curses filled the hum of conversation.

"Cole!" Someone shouted from the back and a chorus of cheers rose up from the group gathered by a pool table.

Cole ushered her toward them. "This is the entire clan, minus Gray." He pointed to the new faces one by one. "Hudson, Sawyer, Nolan. You already met Leah and Callum."

Three big men all rounded the pool table and

tried to ply her with handshakes. The suddenness of it forced her a step back, and Cole immediately placed himself in front of her and set a hand on Nolan's chest. His voice was thick with warning when he spoke. "Don't get any closer. Any of you."

Leah slipped past him and stuck out her hand. "Come perch on the side with me, Riles. These barbarians can do our bidding and fetch our drinks while we shout at them."

Callum took a pull from his beer bottle, then leaned over the table to line up a shot. "How's that different from any other night?"

Leah's lips twitched with a smile. She pulled a cue stick from the wall and nudged Callum in the side right as he took his shot. The ball jumped off the table and rolled on the floor. "Foul! That's what you get for having a smart mouth."

Rylee settled primly next to Leah on a row of stools lining the wall. Away from the others, and with Cole in sight, she relaxed. No one could sneak up behind her, and she was certain Cole would tear anyone apart who tried to hurt her. He made her feel safe enough to enjoy herself in a bar for the first time ever.

He took her order, only making fun of her a tiny bit for wanting a fruity cider, and disappeared in the direction of the bar. Not entirely hidden, she realized. She could see his messy black hair pushing through the crowd, there and back again.

"Where's Gray?" he asked, passing her a bottle with a wink.

"He pulled the short straw for an extra shift," Callum answered and passed him the cue stick. "You're subbing in for me. Can't trust Leah not to commit sabotage."

"What makes you think she'll behave with me?"

"Because she has someone new to impress." Leah fluttered her eyelashes at Rylee.

"I'm impressed," Rylee said. "Sabotage away."

Cole placed his hand over his heart and made a hurt face. "Betrayal!"

The game went on, and she chimed in when she could think of something funny. The Strathorns were rough and crude, but their words were nearly always accompanied by a quick smile and laughing eyes. They gave each other a hard time, but there was a lot of love between them.

She checked regularly on Cole. The tense agitation he had at Hogshead slowly melted away. Being around his clan, joking and slapping hands on shoulders, brightened him up again.

And, she realized, he watched her as much as she

darted glances toward him. They were little looks, flicks of his eyes and a deliberate turning of his body to always keep her in his sight. There was a constant awareness between them, delicate like a spider web, then thicker as the night went on.

Cheeks heating, she barely noticed Leah leaning in and jumped when the other woman spoke.

"A little foxy told me you're coming to brunch with us tomorrow."

Cole shouted over the others, "By the Broken, Leah. You can't go dragging her into your little cabal of mischief makers."

"I can, and I will. I'm humanizing us, which is a shitton more than can be said for these guys." She jerked her thumb toward Nolan and Hudson, who were raising their lips at one another in a snarl.

Callum passed a hand down his face. "No brawling," he ordered. Neither man glanced at him. "No. Brawling."

Leah piped in, "Nolan, I heard Becca doesn't like scars."

Nolan blinked and slashed his eyes to the side. That distraction was enough to ease the tension between them.

Rylee sucked air into her lungs and Leah flashed her a smile. "Sorry about that. Usually it's not so bad for humans. But Callum is the big alpha man and I've got a monster inside me."

"That was you two?" She would give anything to take notes but suspected they wouldn't find it polite. She stashed away the little bits of information for future questions when she had Cole alone.

Leah nodded and waved her empty glass in the air until one of the others pulled it from her hands. "Mhm. It's clan dynamics. The underlings have to submit or it messes with their heads. Good alphas don't ever abuse it because, you know, *good*. And doing wrong things under orders fucks with a person and turns them rotten. Which is why Callum won't ever team up with me to make these baby bears hold dance contests."

Rylee's mouth dropped open. "You can do that? Just order them to do anything?"

Callum jumped in. "Don't listen to her. She wants to believe she can control everyone around her, and we mostly give in because it's easier to deal with a happy Leah than a disappointed, power-hungry Leah. I could force them to shift back and forth, and halt that urge to fight one another. A strong enough will can throw off my control. And none of these guys are going to participate in Bearden's Got Talent just for her."

"Fascinating."

"We are, thank you," Leah said with a single nod. "About time someone recognizes that. So, you're coming to brunch."

Cole dropped a new pint of beer into Leah's hand. He crossed in front of Rylee, temporarily blocking her from Leah and Callum, and planted a quick kiss on her cheek before she could object. She pressed her lips together to keep her smile from getting out of control. It'd been like that all week, from little looks to stolen kisses in the supply closet. Cole was good for her.

Cole pointed the bottom of his beer bottle at Leah but kept his eyes on Rylee. The dark grey swirled with a hint of gold. "She's relentless. Don't feel bad if you need to tell her 'yes' just to get her to shut up."

"No, no. This is nice," she insisted and surprised herself when she reached out and squeezed his hand. Maybe she could be normal. Maybe she stood a chance of fixing herself. He was making a night on the town feel utterly natural.

She couldn't keep her smile from spreading when he gave her another wink and squeezed her fingers back. The beautiful gold of his eyes swirled faster and faster, until all the grey was overtaken. It was gorgeous to watch and left her speechless even when he moved away to take his turn at the pool table.

She knew he didn't want a mate. He said so when he explained a little of the dynamic to her. But they were approaching something big. Something that felt like it deserved a name.

Rylee shook herself after a moment and leaned closer to Leah. "Something that hasn't been made clear. You were human before, and now you're mated and a shifter. Are those things one and the same?"

"Two different types of bites. Here's the difference." Leah crossed an ankle over her knee and hiked up her pant leg. "That's the bite that turned me into a shifter. By a bear to make a bear."

Rylee nodded solemnly. There was a vaguely silver sheen to the jagged scar around her calf.

Leah tugged her jeans back into place, then pulled the collar of her tank top sideways. A smaller, less horrific scar marred her skin where her neck and shoulder met. "And this is the claiming mark. By a shifter to claim their mate. Callum has one, too."

Callum glanced over at the sound of his name. "She only nearly ripped my throat out, but yeah, I've got hers."

"I heard no complaints at the time," she purred

and swiped her finger across the mark on Callum's skin. His eyes closed, and he stifled a groan. He dropped his bottle on the nearest table, then planted a shoulder into Leah's middle and picked her up. She squealed and kicked, but Callum didn't let her loose. "We're heading home. See you good folks tomorrow."

Nolan snorted and rolled his eyes. "Indecent."

Hudson punched him in the shoulder. "Would you *please* get laid? You're starting to sound like my grandmother."

Sawyer crossed his arms over his chest and said blandly, "Maybe he *has* gotten laid and that's exactly why he sounds like Granny."

"Too far, man. Too far," Nolan growled and pushed away from the group.

Hudson shrugged and pointed at them all. "'Nother game?"

"Nah." Sawyer swallowed the last of his pint and set it down with a clink. "I've got a girl to go see."

"Well, I'm out. Later, lovebirds," Hudson announced and left them alone.

Cole quirked an eyebrow at her. "I can drop you off, or walk, whichever you prefer."

After the rowdy evening, the air seemed too silent. She didn't want that silence hanging over her for the rest of the night. Her cheeks hurt from smiling at the clan's ridiculous antics and constant teasing, and that, too, she wasn't ready to relinquish.

Rylee bit her lower lip and worked up the courage to say the words droning in her head. "I don't want to go back to the inn. I don't want the night to end."

His grin split his face, dirty and sexy and happy all at once. He bent down and pressed his lips to her lobe. "Can I take you to my home?"

Rylee swallowed hard. Butterflies shook their wings in her stomach. "Yes."

CHAPTER 15

Cole grabbed Rylee's hand and strode purposefully across the street and into the quiet parking lot of Hogshead. Gruff gentleman that he was, he held open the door and helped her up the step into his truck. She always thought lifted vehicles were silly and unnecessary, but the thing fit Cole. She couldn't imagine him cramming himself behind the wheel of the little compact car she drove at home.

His hand was hot and heavy on her thigh the entire drive away from Hogshead. She started to feel the swell of nerves just as they turned away from the streetlights and down a dark, unpaved road. She bumped along, Cole's hand keeping her steady, until they burst into a clearing and pulled to a stop in front of a dark cabin.

Rylee hopped out of his truck and spun in a slow circle. Lights on other porches revealed the rest of the cabins in the clearing. They were within shouting distance and separated by huge trees and other foliage. Big trucks, all of them, were parked outside of most. More dirt than gravel ringed the clearing but left space in the center for a grill and a handful of chairs and a picnic table.

"I don't usually bring anyone home," Cole said right behind her.

She jumped at his voice, heart thudding in her chest. She turned and raised an eyebrow. "Usually?"

He smirked. "I'm not big into jealousy, little bit. But you make it cute. Come on, I'll show you my den."

He thumped upstairs to a deck, and she was surprised to see a rocking swing in one corner. She was not jealous. She had no right to be jealous. And she certainly wasn't thinking of Cole curled up with some other girl, swinging their summer away.

He turned and rubbed at his nose. "Easy, little bit," he murmured.

A quick twist of his keys pushed open his door,

and he escorted her inside. Her, she reminded herself. No one else was there. It was just them.

Just her, and a massive man who could use all those muscles for misery.

She pushed away the stray thought. Cole had done nothing to harm her. He'd gone out of his way to make her comfortable. Stolen kisses in supply closets and not pressuring her to see to his needs, that was what he offered her. She didn't want to let panic win out against him.

A switch just past the entryway illuminated the kitchen with lights built into the high ceiling. The hideous voice shouting for her to worry and run was banished with the rest of the cabin's darkness.

Work boots and running shoes were lined up by the door. A half moon rug decorated the edge, intended for dirty shoes to kick off the muck from outside. It was as clean as everything else she could see. The kitchen looked spotless, and a couple pillows were stacked neatly in the corners of his couch.

The space was at odds with Cole. He looked wild and ferocious, with dark tresses pushed back in a messy fashion. The tattoos covering his skin didn't pair with the cabin.

"*This* is your place?" she asked.

Oh, he saw the bafflement on her face and it quirked a smile on his lips. "Now you see why I don't bring anyone home. I have a reputation to uphold."

He kicked off his boots and settled them in line with his other shoes. Not knowing what else to do, she did the same. Her sneakers looked tiny by comparison.

Cole stared for a long moment at their shoes lined up next to each other. Then he shook himself and continued leading her into his home, flicking on a pair of lamps on either side of the couch to give the living room a softer glow.

"I need neat and orderly. It helps keep my bear calm," he said, watching her take in details of his life.

She had the distinct impression he was feeling her out and judging her reaction. When she didn't give him anything but a tiny bit of surprise, he relaxed enough to take a seat.

"Tell me about it." She followed him, curling her legs under her and resting an elbow on the back of the couch.

He gave her a look. One where his eyebrows shot together and his lips curled up into a smile. It said he had no worries, to ask him no questions, that everything was just fine in his life. That look was a well-practiced lie. She had one of her own that she gave to everyone over the years. It stung to be on the other side.

"Please?" She reached out and placed her hand on his shoulder before he could give her the denial that followed that sort of look. "I'm asking as a—your—"

Oh, she was mucking everything up. She didn't know how to handle the ambiguous, tenuous, *thing* that had grown between them. She hurried on, ignoring her flushing cheeks. "I'm not doing research here. I shared with you. You can do the same with me."

"Will you come here?" He patted his thighs and tilted his head in invitation. "Touch me, and you can have all my secrets."

"That's a big promise," she said. Her heart sank onto the wings of butterflies that made up her stomach and she shifted once more. From the couch, to straddling him, with heat slithering through her veins.

Cole pressed her hands against his chest, holding them flat while his eyes slid closed. "My bear is restless. Unsettled. He wants to fight all the fucking time, and it doesn't matter if it's with me or with anyone else. I used to have everything sorted out and knew where I belonged. Then Pop got sick and Callum took over in the mayor's office for a time, which meant I had to step up in the firehouse. It was a hard time for everyone and all that uncertainty made my bear nuts. But he was a damn beast even before then."

His throat worked with his swallow and he slid his hands to her thighs. She kept contact with him, sliding her hands up and down his chest. Even through his shirt, she felt ripples of muscle. She stroked up and down, drawing tiny noises from him that curled pleasure hotly in her middle.

"Schedules, hard labor," he continued, voice thick. "Those work. If I know what I'm doing and when, or tire myself out so there's no fight left, I can have a little peace. He won't rip at my insides and roar for blood."

How many days had she worked herself to exhaustion? How many nights did she stay awake with memories she didn't want to keep? His words could have come out of her mouth.

"Being around you, that's the best solution. I'm not aching to tear into someone or seconds away from shifting. You quiet the animal inside me. You make me feel calm." He raised his eyes to hers. "You're not running. You don't even smell afraid."

"You make me feel brave." She balled her hands into his shirt and pressed her mouth to his. He groaned and parted his lips, taking control as soon as she gave the smallest sign that she wouldn't back away. He wanted her consent in everything before he would let his control slip and it drove her wild.

Darcy gave her a way out of Bearden, but she'd be crazy to take her up on the offer. Crazy to leave behind her research, but most of all, crazy to leave Cole. He'd dug his way into her heart and past all her defenses. He claimed a part of her that she'd unwillingly shared with someone else. Instead of wanting to run, she wanted more. She wanted normal. She wanted to feel whole.

She slid her palms up his shirt. He was hot to the touch. That soothed tight muscles up and down her body.

God, he made her feel drunk. She'd barely had anything to drink with dinner and only toyed with a bottle of cider at the bar. It was all Cole. He was the one making her head swim and daring her on.

He pulled away, eyes finding hers. "What is it you want, little bit?"

"I feel the same as you and your bear. You make me feel calm and normal." Rylee licked her lips and pressed her forehead to his. "I can't guarantee I won't freak out, but I want to try for more."

Relief, victory, and joy all played out in his eyes

before they finally settled into molten, hungry gold. He brought his lips to hers again, kissing her softly. Testing and teasing at the same time. He wanted to see if she'd run, but she held firm.

A delicious groan rumbled in his chest and vibrated through her. He wound his arms around her, one hand going to the back of her neck and the other digging into her hip. He pulled her into his sphere and against the hard planes of his body, showing exactly how much he wanted her with a directed rock of her hips.

He was big and thick everywhere. Instead of frightening her, she wanted to sink into him. Let him wrap around her and keep her safe from every threat imaginable. He'd already pushed the broken pieces of her back together and now he was handing her the glue to keep herself whole.

Cole dragged his mouth over her skin, nipping at her neck. "This stops wherever you want. Understand me? The moment you smell of fear, the first time you breathe a hint of no, I stop."

He kissed her between his words, nipped her flesh, sucked her and rubbed his stubbled cheek into the crook of her neck. Rylee nodded and even more weight lifted off her shoulders.

The world shifted as Cole stood. He carried her

easily from his couch and into a dark bedroom. Excitement started her heart tripping in her chest. She'd met his lips and let him slide his fingers inside her. She could push her boundaries just a little bit further. And she trusted him when he said he'd stop the moment she stepped a toe over the line she wasn't sure still existed.

Trust. It was such an odd thing to find in an even odder place. She never thought she'd be working with the supernatural, or falling for one.

Cole dropped her to the bed, then left her to turn on lights before she could even ask. He was all about her comfort, and she couldn't see in the dark like he could. She appreciated the gesture; she wanted to ground herself in him and not let ghosts in the dark terrify her into stopping.

He knelt on the floor between her legs and ran his fingertips slowly up her ankle, up her shin, lightly over her knees. He pressed his palms against her thighs and skimmed higher and curled his fingers around her waist. He hesitated slightly, with his fingers heating the small of her back and his eyes boring into her. When she didn't flinch, he dragged her shirt up and over her head.

"Do you know what happens next? What I'm going to do to you and make you feel?" Cole's touch was fire blazing a path back down her body and to the front of her jeans. He held her eyes when his fingers worked open the button, then dragged down her zipper.

Brave. He made her brave. And stupidly hot as he rolled her jeans down her legs. Still, her cheeks flamed red. "I know how sex and foreplay work. I've watched porn before."

A growl rumbled in his chest and he turned hungry eyes on her. "Tell me. What did you like?"

"When they, and you, ah..."

He leaned into her, his thumbs stroking the place where her legs met her body. Slowly dipping toward her center and slowly teasing her. "I have to hear you say the words, little bit. Need to know it's what you want."

She melted just a bit more. He was perfect. "I liked when you used your fingers on me. And I liked knowing you wanted to taste me. I want you to start here." She pushed a palm up her body and cupped her breast.

Cole mirrored the motion on her other side, gold eyes dropping to her chest and a growl on his tongue. He reached behind her and skillfully unsnapped her bra and then she was bare for him. His growl grew louder in her ears, but it didn't fill her with fear. She wanted more and he was there to oblige.

She arched into his touch and her hand fell away when he leaned forward to pull her nipple between his lips. He cupped and squeezed her breast, lapping and licking her nipple, until her mouth fell open with a soft moan.

He moved to her other breast, repeating his ministrations. His free hand ran down her ribs and raised the fine hairs all over her body with his delicate touch. Over her waist, squeezing her hip. Rylee sucked in a breath when his fingers eased under the edge of her panties and dipped into her center.

Rylee turned her head into her shoulder and mewled something high and breathy. God above, he was overwhelming her in the best way possible. She didn't have time to think of anything else when he was steadily building pleasure in her.

He released her nipple with a wet pop and then his hair tickled her thighs. Air exploded out of her lips and liquid heat slicked her core. He dipped his fingers into her and followed that up with a long, slow lick that made her eyelids flutter shut.

"Even better than I imagined," Cole groaned between strokes of his tongue.

Shivers rippled up and down her spine. His

words tethered her to the world, otherwise she'd float right away.

He plunged his fingers into her, no longer teasing. Each relentless stroke left her trembling. One swipe of his tongue after another crashed unbelievable pleasure over her. She wanted to drown in it. She never wanted it to end.

"Cole," she panted, loving that his name on her lips drew a growl out of him. He made her feel like the sexiest creature alive, acting like he wanted to do nothing more than taste her and touch her.

Deeper. Faster. Harder. And then she exploded. Her moan morphed into a sudden cry and she arched hard against him. He growled when her hands dug into his hair, pushing his tongue deep inside as she throbbed hard.

"You okay?" Cole asked, kissing a trail up her body. He swallowed hard. His voice was too thick, too full of his bear. He didn't want to intimidate her. He wanted her as relaxed as she'd been in the throes of her release. Fuck, he wanted her head thrown back and his name burning her lips as he buried himself again and again inside her.

But she stiffened when he rose from between her legs and pressed her back against the bed. The faintest whiff of fear entered the cloud of her arousal and soured the mood. Oh, his cock was still hard as a fucking rock and he was desperate to be wrong about that stinging scent, but the silence lengthened and scared the shit out of him.

Bear roaring in his head and wanting to go to war with the world to kill everyone who might give Rylee a frown, Cole rolled to his back and pulled her across his thighs. They'd found the line and he wouldn't push her, just as he promised. He liked this position better. He could watch her, touch her, gauge her reaction.

"You're perfect. This is perfect," he assured her. "You're in control."

Another pensive silence and he wanted to kick himself. She was backing away, shutting down on him. He wanted to wedge himself in that door she'd cracked open. Show her the world wasn't as dark as she'd been taught.

"You're wearing too many clothes," she finally said, biting her lower lip.

Cole searched her face. Big, blue eyes stared back at him under disheveled bangs. That stinging hint of fear faded fast and sweet, sexy arousal once again filled his nose.

He leaned up and ripped his shirt over his head, not needing to be told twice when his mate wanted him.

He couldn't even push back on his bear leaking the wrong words into his head. She was his. She belonged in his bed, in his den. And he belonged in her.

He urged Rylee up just enough for him to shove his pants down his thighs. Arrogant pride filled his chest at her sucked in breath when he unsheathed his cock. "Like what you see, little bit?" he smirked.

Oh, she did. Her eyes went wide and her tongue flicked out to wet her lips.

"Touch me," he ordered.

She wrapped her hand around his shaft and stroked him up and down.

Cole fell back, pillowing his head on his arms. She was so fucking hot with her hair bouncing around her shoulders and her glasses tilted just slightly out of place. But most of all, her hands ringing his dick made him throb.

"I'm in control, right?" She leaned forward, hair tickling his chest. Another stroke of his cock and she kissed the tip of his nose.

Holy fuck. He liked being in control. He needed it. But she could boss him around the bedroom all she wanted if she kept looking at him with those sultry eyes. He nodded.

"I want you inside me." She licked her lips again and pushed down that tiny flicker of uncertainty. And with it gone, she rose up on her knees and fit his head against her entrance.

Cole thought he was going to die. His heart thumped as fast as hers as she slid slowly over him, eyes closed and a tiny, sexy smile lifting her lips. She sucked in a shuddering breath the moment she settled against him. Her eyes popped open a second later, and she reversed her path.

Fuck, she was tight. And wet. And hot. He was already addicted to the sensation of her gripping his dick. This was a bad, terrible, best fucking idea in the world.

He rose up, abs flexing with the movement. He closed an arm around her, hand cupping her shoulder and dragging her back down his shaft. He guided her movements, showed her how to ride him. "Do you know how good you feel?" he mouthed against her throat.

"Do you?" Her tiny laugh morphed into a moan on his next thrust.

CECILIA LANE

By the Broken, she was fun to fuck. He needed someone who would laugh with him one moment and pant his name the next. Sex needed to be fun and hot and sweaty and—

"Cole," she moaned again and had his entire attention.

Her mouth fell open, and she tightened around him. He guided her up and down his cock, short, shallow thrusts designed to bump her clit when their hips bucked together. She trembled, tiny little shakes as pleasure built inside her. Red flushed her cheeks and spread down her neck and across her chest.

He leaned forward and sucked a nipple between his lips, spilling another mewling moan into the air. His balls drew up tight against his body and he knew he was as close as she was to going off. He wanted to feel her pulsing around him.

"Mine," he growled, just as her head fell back with a silent cry. She tightened around him, squeezing him in the most intimate embrace possible, and he emptied himself in her with a roar of his own.

He pressed his lips to her neck, right where a claiming mark would go, and barely wound a chain around his bear before he set his fangs against her flesh.

Close. Too fucking close. Too tempting. Too fucking perfect.

He smoothed her hair away from her face, kissing her lips and cheeks and nose. He settled her glasses back where they belonged. She breathed hard and heavy, and he scented the air again and again.

No fear.

CHAPTER 16

Cole sucked air down his lungs and took the bottle of water from Callum with gratitude. After a swig, he ducked his head under the nearby waterfall and scrubbed his hair clean. The fresh water felt good on his skin after running the border deep into the mountains.

Leah had caught Rylee sneaking out of his cabin that morning and insisted on being the one to aid her walk of shame before they met up with the Holden sisters for brunch. Cole almost pitied Pierre for the storm of squealing that was about to hit his restaurant.

With nothing better to do, he agreed to run a section of the border with Callum. The first half would be in their human forms, then they'd head home on four paws. And maybe by then, Leah and her band of troublemakers would release Rylee from their clutches and he could have her to himself again. His bear rumbled an agreement.

Rylee hadn't been able to sleep naked, which was a loss. That she stayed the night and slept in a shirt of his was a win in his book. A very sexy, very delicious win.

"You're thinking about her again," Callum teased.

Cole shook his head and sent droplets of water flying everywhere. "Fuck off. Am not."

"Your pheromones are going haywire and fucking hell, man. Keep that thing hidden." Callum raised his hand to block Cole from the waist down.

"I say again. Fuck. Off." Cole raised his middle finger toward his brother and adjusted his pants. He wasn't *that* hard.

He was glad Callum insisted on them running. He hadn't spent much time with the clan while he was following Rylee around and making sure she was safe. Or spying, if he gave Olivia's job description any heed. Regardless, his bear felt a touch more relaxed now that they'd burnt off a bunch of energy in the presence of their alpha.

Not only that, but he was happy to spend time with his brother. Callum filled many roles in his life and the clan, so it was a rare treat for just the two of them to do something together. Not that he'd ever breathe a fucking word to Callum or any of the others in the clan. He knew where the line was between acceptable and sappy behavior. Callum could follow Leah around with big moon eyes, but Cole wouldn't be accused of being tied to his brother's apron strings.

Cole took a seat on a nearby bench and took a look around while Callum doused himself in the cool water. The trees were in full bloom and the water looked gorgeous rushing down the side of the mountain. There was a reason why many in Bearden used the area as a romantic date spot. Maybe he should make plans to bring Rylee.

"How did you know, with Leah? How did you know she wasn't just some human and you wanted to mate her?"

"You know how it is. Your beast takes notice and hates you every moment you don't let him near the woman. You can't breathe without her, and it's even harder when you're near. Instinctive urges to protect and provide."

"Yeah, but, how did you *know*? Leah was human. It's different. It's... She wasn't part of our life."

Callum clapped a hand on his shoulder and

pulled the bottle from his hands. He refilled it under the waterfall, sliding a glance toward Cole while he waited. "My bear knew before me. Started sending me all these images of Leah with both a mate mark and a bite mark. I couldn't stop thinking about her. Couldn't wait to be near her again. And the thought of her leaving, on her own or because of her asshole fae ex, drove me mad. I was ready to follow her out of the enclave, if that's what she wanted."

"Do you think Mom and Pop were mates?"

Callum shook his head. "No. He wouldn't have let her go and she wouldn't have left him if they were. They'd have found a way to work things out. Mom just wasn't meant for this world."

It was truer than Callum even knew, Cole thought sourly. He pushed away painful thoughts before they could overwhelm him or piss off his bear. Their mother had left them when they were still just babies. She made it clear they weren't worthy of her love.

But Callum did ease his mind. If his bear was right and she was his mate, they would find a way out of the quicksand that existed all around them.

"Come on," Callum said. "I want to show you something." Callum jogged up the path to the bridge that passed in front of the waterfall. Cole growled and followed after.

It was a short distance away that Callum stepped off the path. Cole frowned. He thought he knew where Callum was taking them, and every step made him more certain. There was a small cave nearby that opened into a hidden valley of sorts. The Strathorns used it for some ridiculous clan bonding camping that his father forced on them when they were younger. That'd been before he lost his head and Callum had to take over.

Cole followed Callum through the familiar cave path and right back into the sun on the other side. He opened his mouth to give his brother shit and ask if he needed a banjo for some camp side tunes when he noticed other people already in the clearing.

Gideon Bloodwing and his clan of dragons lounged through most of the space. One of them even sunned himself in dragon form. Gray, his Strathorn clansman, huddled unhappily on the edge.

"What's wrong, Gray? The fire breathers not being warm and friendly?" Cole called out.

All heads turned toward him and Callum. Gray didn't move except to throw a middle finger into the air.

Gideon pushed off a cot where he'd been laying

and crossed toward him. Two nearly identical men followed, and even the dragon opened an eye and watched.

Gideon's beard had grown thicker since the last time Cole saw the man. Everything had changed that night when Bearden was attacked by a visiting delegation of fae. Their leader had crazy ideas of using the Broken to tear a new hole through the veil between worlds. It was Gideon's fire that saved both Callum and Leah's lives.

And, ultimately, that night brought Rylee into the enclave. The crazed fae had a contingency in case his plans were defeated. He taped an interview with a local newscaster that revealed the enclaves protected by the Broken's magic, and the supernatural folk living in the hidden towns.

Cole hated the fae man for what he'd done and was glad that Gideon burned him down to nothing. But he didn't hate that Rylee had become twisted in his life. Silver linings and all that hippy-dippy shit.

He knew Gideon had called in his Bloodwings that night, and knew there was tension between them. He never expected Callum to aid in hiding them within Bearden territory.

"So this is where you've been hiding out." Cole clasped Gideon's hand and drew him in for a quick hug. "You better get back to town soon. Leah's going to take over the Roost."

Worry lined Gideon's face. The Roost, in all its grimy glory, was his baby. Leah wormed her way into first cleaning the floors and tables, then fixing the burnt out lights. "She hasn't changed anything, has she? Customers are still coming in?"

"Relax," Callum said. "She's taking care of the place just fine. She hasn't chased anyone off, hasn't mauled anyone over a tab, hasn't redecorated. Your office might be a little more pink and glittery when you get back, but that's it. No difference."

"Pink? Glittery?" Gideon scowled. "What did she do?"

Cole blew out a breath. "Nothing. Yet. He's just kidding. But she does have a gallon of pink paint stashed away for some purpose we aren't sure of yet. So, you might want to get back soon."

One of the men behind Gideon stepped into the circle. "Can we get on with this?"

Gideon stiffened with every word and the scent of burning wood reached Cole's nose. "Right. We've been flying and monitoring the activity around the camps from above."

"How? Orders were not to go near them, human or military alike." Cole's brows shot together. He'd heard nothing from Rylee about Major Delano being irritated, and certainly nothing from Olivia about needing to closely watch the situation.

The other dragon grinned, but it wasn't a friendly expression. "We won't be seen. Trust us. You groundlings don't know all our secrets."

Gideon tongued his teeth. "What Damien means is that we can make ourselves hidden, like the enclaves. It's part of our magic."

Damien crossed his arms over his chest and stared at Gideon with flinty eyes. "Do you always reveal the secrets of our people to the groundlings?"

Gideon rounded on the man. "Our people? You must be referring to everyone with ancestors that stepped through the veil. Fae, vampires, and shifters of all shapes are our people. I know you're not bringing that dragon clan *bullshit* into my enclave. You're here to help Bearden. If you don't want to do that, you're welcome to leave."

Damien's eyes blazed with fury, but he raised his hands up and backed away a step. Gideon stared him down for several long seconds before turning back to Callum and Cole. "They're mapping the border. It started with walking the path you and the human marked up, but they've expanded on it. They're dipping in and sending up drones, too."

"So they have people with supernatural blood. That's no surprise. At least one of them saw us when we introduced ourselves," Callum said.

"That's not all." Gideon scrubbed a hand through his hair and then spat on the ground. "They got a shifter with them."

The silence beat down on all of them. The distant cawing of a bird brought them back to focus.

"What do you mean?"

"Exactly what I said. They got a shifter. Doused up in cologne strong enough we can smell it in the skies, but the scent of fur is still underneath."

Callum nodded like he wasn't surprised. "Keep watch and see if you can find out who they have. It's probably not someone from Bearden. Let them keep at it with the drones and mapping. It's going to draw more attention and show we're watching if accidents start to happen."

Gideon dropped his voice. "Not sure how long these ones will stay without any action."

Callum nodded. "I know. Do the best you can. You're our eyes right now." He dipped over to Gray for a quick word, then strode past Cole.

Head stuck processing everything he'd just seen and overheard, he trailed after Callum. It wasn't until they were back through the cave and out of earshot that he spoke. The beginnings of anger were working their way into existence. "That's what you wanted to show me? You're working with the Blood-wings? I assume Olivia doesn't know."

"You'd be wrong. She knows. She's new, and I don't fully trust her, but she has Bearden's best interests in mind. This is our insurance that the other enclaves know what's happening on our borders. I don't think Gideon expected his dragons to show, and we're going to use them while they're here."

"I knew they were in the enclave, but damn, Callum. You're dragging a whole mess on our heads."

"That fucker Jamin dragged this on us when he announced our existence to the entire world," Callum growled. He stopped suddenly and turned on Cole. "I know you're interested in that girl, but you need to watch yourself."

"Like you did with Leah?" Cole's lips twisted into a sour shape. "You forget, *alpha*, I heard what Bruce said about her being planted here by the fae. I brought you that warrant for murder with her name on it. I didn't say anything before because there wasn't any point. She got turned, and she's one of us now. But if one human can be brought into the fold, why not another? I don't see any other solution, honestly. We have a fucking circus camping out next to the guys pointing guns at us. We're not going to be able to hide this place."

"That's not the same. Leah was on the run and got pushed into the enclave. Rylee is here to study us like we're lab rats."

Cole snarled. "Is that what's all of this is about? Olivia invited a human into our borders, when you'd do your best to keep them out? You're not so different from the new mayor, you know. You both push me toward Rylee, then tell me to hold myself back. *Push, Cole. Pull, Cole. Watch out for her, Cole.* I'm fucking sick of it. She doesn't want to hurt us. If she knew something, she'd say."

"Are you sure about that? And what if they're keeping secrets from her? What could she find out for us?"

"No." Cole shook his head to cut off that line of thinking before it even started. His brother's words were sounding too much like Olivia's. "We're not heading down that path. I'm not putting her in danger to find some tiny, useless nugget of information."

Callum opened his mouth to argue further, but Cole's phone rang shrilly in his pocket. "You going to get that?" Callum asked. "Might be your mate."

Cole spun on his heel to avoid throwing a punch

in his brother's stupid face and pulled out the soft bag he would use to store his clothes when he shifted to his bear for the run home. His phone was next, and he managed to answer on the last ring. "What?"

"Where the hell are you and your idiot brother?"

Cole held the phone away from his ear to save his sensitive hearing from Olivia's screeches. "We're out. What's gone wrong?"

"That damn Major Delano has gone off his rocker! Doctor Garland has been released from her contract and they're clearing out her lab as we speak!" Olivia ground her teeth hard enough to be heard over the phone. "You were supposed to watch for this, Strathorn. Why am I hearing about the military entering our enclave after they've already done so?"

Fuck, fuck, fuck. That job meant everything to Rylee. And Delano, that asshole, wanted her gone. He didn't think Rylee expected Delano to interfere. Which meant she'd been kept in the dark. There was danger in the military camp keeping any information secret.

"I'm on my way."

CHAPTER 17

"Look who showed up!" Becca squealed and stuffed herself into the booth with her sister right behind her.

"Look who's talking," Leah grumbled. She pushed the pitcher of mimosas toward the sisters. "We've been waiting five minutes. Five! Do you know how many passes Pierre has done?"

"At least ten," Rylee giggled. "I couldn't keep count. Does he think we're going to do a dine-and-dash or steal the silverware?"

"Probably. You just don't know what sorts of criminality we get up to in our inferior places of business," Becca snorted.

"How are you?" Faith asked.

"Great. Wonderful." Rylee smiled with her answer. Neither of those words fit or described how she truly felt.

How was she? She felt like she'd ingested all the alcohol and drugs she missed out on in college, though she'd never made herself available for that crowd to notice and invite her anywhere. She felt like she could do ten million action scenes all on her own and all in a row. She could swallow the world and every last bit of terribleness in it.

Cole was helping her turn her entire worldview on its head. He couldn't undo the years of hiding and wishing she'd done anything else that night, but he was easing her into living around her damage. She could shove it all in a dark corner of her mind and forget about it when she had him to lean on. He made her feel invincible.

"I caught this one doing the walk of shame," Leah piped up.

"Oooh," Faith and Becca said at the same time.

Rylee lifted her chin. "I'm a grown woman. I don't need to feel ashamed of anything that may have transpired last night."

"Damn." Becca whistled. "The Strathorns are on a roll with you newbies. Which one is going to be next?"

"Nolan," Leah whispered to her mimosa. She raised innocent eyes. "It's not like I've been sending romantically named drinks to you both for my own fun."

"Sex on the beach, slippery nipple, big banana daiquiri, and pink panty dropper are not romantic drinks." Becca ticked off a finger with each drink name. "And you're insane if you think they will get me to talk to that man."

Leah cupped her chin and stared into nothing. "Pink panty dropper night was a fun night. You almost said three words to Nolan."

"'Fuck off' doesn't count as talking."

Faith wrapped an arm around her sister's shoulder. "Enough about Nolan. I want to hear about Cole."

Rylee could feel her cheeks turning a rosy shade. Cole said he thought her blushes were sexy, and that thought added another degree of red.

The entire night had gone beyond well. Even the little kerfuffle between Olivia and Cole hadn't ruined everything. She'd had dinner, drinks, and gone home with him. She even worked up the courage to stay the night! Not that there'd been much room for objections. Cole certainly kept her mind occupied on anything but feeling nervous.

He'd been such a sexy gentleman. He knew even before she did when he pushed her too far and immediately scaled back to distracting kisses and touches. Rylee pressed her thighs together. Thinking about his hands and lips all over her body made her eager to see him again.

"And that, my friends, is the look of one falling down the rabbit hole of lust to the land of love," Leah announced.

Rylee opened her mouth to deny, deny, deny. It'd been one night and Cole didn't want a mate, which meant there was nothing permanent to be found with him. She'd leave Bearden eventually, and she'd be left with extremely fond memories of the man who helped make her feel less broken.

But then her phone chirped and distracted her. She tugged the device from her pocket, brows drawing together in confusion at the notification. One of the security measures put into place was a keypad lock on the lab door that would notify her of any uses. She was the only one in Bearden with the code and she was very much not at the clinic.

"It's my lab. Someone accessed the room." She stood quickly. "I need to go. Sorry."

"Hold up, I'll go with you. You'll get there faster

driving than walking," Leah answered. Quick good-byes were exchanged with Becca and Faith, then they were out the door and loading into Leah's truck. She didn't have time to worry about Leah's speeding before they arrived.

"Those your guys?" Leah asked, pulling to a stop on the side of the street next to the clinic.

Three dark green military trucks took up most of the parking lot. Two men leaned against them with huge guns slung across their chests and bored looks on their faces. At least, until they spotted her and Leah. Then one of them marched in their direction.

Rylee shook her head. "I wasn't told about this."

"Well, fuck. Ring up the mayor. I'll call Callum. This doesn't feel right."

The soldier rapped on the window. "Ma'am, I'm going to need you to move along."

Leah pressed her phone to her ear. "Sorry, can't hear you. I'm on a call."

The soldier continued to argue with Leah while Rylee connected her call. Leah huffed, "No answer."

Rylee had more luck with her call. "Mayor Gale said she'd be right over."

She balled her hands into her lap and tried to see what was being carried to the waiting trucks. Boxes, one after another, were being loaded inside. And the soldier at Leah's window still demanded they move.

She was out the door with Leah jumping after. She couldn't wait. They were tearing apart her lab and possibly ruining everything she'd worked for. If she was being required to relocate the lab, she needed to be the one to pack and facilitate the move. She didn't trust anyone without a degree in the field to handle the samples and equipment she worked with on a daily basis. Heck, she didn't trust anyone but herself to keep everything straight and organized the way she preferred.

"What is going on here?" she demanded as soon as she ducked around the swarm of men carrying away her work and entered the lab itself.

Boxes were lined up on every available surface. Major Brant Delano leaned against a wall and watched the action. Many hands were loading equipment and notes and other supplies with hardly any care for banging around sensitive and expensive items. She winced when a case of slides crashed to the ground and scattered all over the floor.

Her heart thudded in her chest when she recognized the tall man directing the packing. Peter Glasser, the man of her nightmares. He made her a statistic when she did everything right. She went to the police, she reported the crime. But he laid the groundwork and turned her accusation into a he-said, she-said that went utterly nowhere. And with her degree in hand and a recruiter luring her to Nevada, she just let everything go. She wanted to put Peter behind her and forget that terrible night.

And now he was standing in front of her and ripping her world apart all over again.

Her entire body trembled and her voice shook, but she pushed the words out of her mouth. She was done letting him control her through fear and pain. He'd done enough damage. Her short time in Bearden proved she wasn't as weak and broken as she thought.

"Stop. Stop everything. You have no right to be here."

Peter turned and plastered a warm smile on his face. She wanted to punch his teeth out. "Rylee. I was wondering when you'd arrive. There have been some changes that you need to be made aware of."

Delano gloated from a corner. "You're due back in Nevada for a debriefing. Collect your things."

"Excuse me? You do not get to order me around like a child," she snapped.

"The Director thought it best if someone else took over the field work. Major Delano and I have previously worked together and won't butt heads," Peter explained, raising his hands and speaking quietly like she needed soothing. It only made her angrier.

Peter's arrival was a nightmare. He didn't care about the shifters and other supernaturals of Bearden. He didn't think of them as people. He would do more damage than good and jeopardize all of Bearden. A chill worked up and down her spine to think of all the bullheaded bias Peter would bring into the study.

She glared at Peter. "So I'm fired. That's what this is. Delano felt threatened by someone smarter than him, though I'm sure the first squirrel I see outside could give him a run for his money. So he got me kicked out and replaced by someone who will run this project into the ground."

Major Delano's face went from angry red to furious purple. He stomped across the room and brought their noses together with a snarl on his lips. "Get your shit and get out."

"I'm fired, remember? You have zero jurisdiction over me. I'm just a civilian now."

"You can't stay here without permission," Peter interjected. He kept his words calm, but his eyes were cold and dead. That look meant hurt would follow. She didn't want to be left alone with him.

"Neither can you, and I doubt Mayor Gale will instruct the enclave's citizens to be as friendly to you as they were to me once she hears about this."

Peter smirked. "I can be quite persuasive."

Leah crossed her arms over her chest and arched an eyebrow. "I'm not feeling very persuaded. In fact, I'm not feeling very generous, either. I'd like to see your invitation into Bearden. As far as I'm aware, Rylee here was the one requested, not whoever you are."

Several of the soldiers shifted uneasily, some even moving their hands closer to their guns. Rylee felt sick with worry. With trigger-happy soldiers led by a man with a chip on his shoulder, it would only be a matter of time before something disastrous happened. It was exactly the scenario she wanted to prevent.

And she backed down. She didn't want Leah hurt because the woman wanted to defend her. She didn't want to be left alone with Peter or Delano. Most of all, she didn't want to color the people of Bearden as even worse than they'd already been deemed.

"Leah, let's go," she muttered.

"You need to get out of the enclave," Delano ordered.

"She's my guest and she can stay as long as she wants. Unless you want to try physically removing her?" Leah lifted her chin in a challenge just as Callum and Cole shadowed the doorway with Olivia Gale between them.

"What is the meaning of this?" Olivia asked, pushing her way front and center. "I was promised that we would be made aware of anyone crossing our borders."

Peter didn't answer, simply turned and collected some paperwork from a clipboard. "Rylee Garland has been removed from this project. I've been sent to replace her."

"So I've been told." Olivia scanned the paper quickly. "And you are...? Besides obviously unaware of prior agreements."

"Peter Glasser. It will be a pleasure to work with you."

Cole stiffened at the name. Fury and gold colored his eyes when he lifted them to her. "Him?"

Rylee shook her head to stave off the outburst. "Cole, don't. Please."

He blinked. Once, twice. The gold of his eyes faded, but the white-hot fury remained. He bored holes into Peter while the activity resumed. She followed Olivia, Leah, Callum, and Cole out into the hallway and watched box after box disappear.

Delano shoved past with Peter on his heels. He jerked his chin in Cole's direction. "Watch this one. He's trouble."

CHAPTER 18

Rylee sipped at her drink and stared into empty air. Just hours before, she'd been at the top of her game. Running her own lab, even if she reported back to a different facility. Making friends. Falling for a man who showed her nothing but kindness once she pushed back his prickly exterior.

And then it all crashed down around her. She'd need to leave Bearden, and wouldn't have a job to go back to. Leaving meant abandoning her new friends and healing heart.

She thought she was in shock, but then figured she was too angry. None of the tears she expected even dampened the corners of her eyes.

Lost. That was the right word. She felt lost and in limbo with no idea which way to turn.

The couch cushion shifted as Cole took a seat and draped an arm over her shoulder. At least he'd stopped pacing and dragging his hands through his hair. He looked downright murderous with a snarl on his lips and flashing gold eyes. "You can get another job."

She shook her head sadly and tightened a blanket around her shoulders. She wasn't the slightest bit cold, especially with Cole so near, but she took comfort from the added bit of covering. "It doesn't work like that. I'm in a highly competitive field. Research positions are scarce. My references will be checked and triple checked, and as soon as they see I was requested to leave by Delano, they'll want to know more. And as soon as someone talks to that man, I'm toast. I'll be blacklisted as soon as he says the first word about being uncooperative and putting his men in danger. Reputation is everything, and I doubt I'll have one left by morning."

"Well, what do you want to do?"

"Honestly?" She hesitated and toyed with the edge of the blanket. She thought she had more time. A week of stolen kisses and a night of passion wasn't enough. She wasn't ready to give him up. "I want to stay here. With you."

There was a beat before he said anything. One heartbeat, one breath of air, a blink of the eye. A silence that made her hold her breath. Then he spoke.

"You're not meant for this place."

Rylee nodded once and refused to meet his eyes. It was a rejection she could have predicted. He didn't want a mate, and that obviously covered anything in the relationship category. They had fun while it lasted, she told herself. She tried to ignore the pain slashing at her heart.

She twisted out from under his arm. "I should go."

Cole growled and tugged his fingers through his hair again. He looked like a man at odds with himself. "You're good. You can get hurt. You've seen some of my scars. That's the life I have. If I'm not fighting with someone in the clan, then it's someone down at the Roost. If it's not that, then there's the threat of fire when I go back to the firehouse."

"That's no different than outside the enclave," she pointed out. "I could get into a car accident. Or develop a new allergy. I'm already allergic to peni- cillin, did you know that? Not enough to kill me, but

I get swollen and itchy." Heck, she was letting her tongue show her nerves. "There's potential for danger everywhere, is what I mean to say. That's just the price of living."

"Humans aren't meant to stay here. So you'll leave. Now or later, but you'll leave. You'll start your perfect little human family and forget this place."

Rylee frowned. That wasn't the argument she expected. She thought he'd fall back on not wanting to tie himself down, which she could understand. Logically, anyway. Her heart was another matter.

But instead of his using his objections, he was turning it on her. It threw her out of sorts. "Why are you so sure I'd leave?"

"Because that's how it works, Rylee. My mother did it. Humans aren't meant for this life and all the violence involved. We're a strange, small town. And you. You're smart. You're too good for this place. You're too good for me. I'm not worth sticking around for."

She raised her hands to her mouth. He never mentioned his mother. Just him and his brother and his father. One tiny sentence explained so much. "Your mother abandoned you?"

"I don't want to talk about that," he growled again.

He tugged at her heartstrings and kept her tethered to the couch. Whatever happened between them seemed suddenly small in comparison. Cole hid his broken pieces well, but they were still poking at him.

She reached for him slowly and placed her hand on his arm. The connection zinged straight through her and tied her to him. She wanted to hear his story and put his pieces back together, the same way he'd helped her. "Cole, let me in. You shouldered my burdens. I want to return the favor."

Cole's lips twisted into a sour shape. His eyes flared gold, then faded back to grey, then went gold again. He was absolutely fighting with himself, and she wasn't sure which side won for a long moment.

"Pop brought her here after he was outside the enclave for a spell. The only reason it was allowed was because she was pregnant with Callum. He's born, a year goes by, and then I came along. She left shortly after. And that's the end of the story as far as Callum is concerned."

"But not for you?"

"Not for me, no. I'm the dumbass that can't let anything lie. It itches at me until I get to the bottom of the problem. Callum says it makes me a good second to his alpha. I dig and poke and bother until we're all getting along for a few hours. The others say it makes me an obnoxious asshole."

Rylee huffed a laugh. She recognized the deflection in his self-deprecating humor and while she let him have a moment, she still wanted to know more. He seemed to sense it, too. He leaned up and rested his forearms on his thighs. The floor under his feet held his attention, but he finally spoke again.

"It was after high school and I didn't know what to do with my life. A couple friends were heading off to college outside the enclave, Callum was working as a probie in the firehouse under Pop. I didn't know who I was supposed to be. I got curious about my mother and the stories of why she left. I guess you could say I was looking for some kindred spirit.

"I found her in a town not much bigger than Bearden, so it wasn't the size that bothered her. It was me and Callum and Pop. She didn't want anything to do with us. You see, she'd moved on. Had her perfect little human family. Human husband. Human kids just starting high school. She was happy. And when she realized who I was, she went crazy. Called me freak and demon and devil, threatened to shoot me in the face if I didn't leave her alone."

Oh, she could see him clearly. Big, tough man

insistent on remaining aloof and uncomplicated. Once anything looked too serious, he bolted before he could get hurt. Something was rotten with him if his own mother didn't want him.

He couldn't be more wrong.

She shifted and straddled his lap, then wrapped her arms around his neck. "You're worth loving. You're not a terrible creature. It was her choice to leave. You didn't drive her away."

"You really believe that, don't you?" At her nod, he let go of a rough sigh that verged on a growl. "Rylee, I've done shit that I'm not proud of. Being a shifter means I live a violent life and my bear is only getting worse. Does that sound like someone who doesn't drive others away?"

"Yes." His eyes dipped to her lips, and she slowly, slowly leaned into him.

The first brush of her lips against his rattled another growl in his chest. Cole tugged her closer. Each gentle stroke firmed her resolve. She could find herself in Bearden. She could put herself back together with Cole to lean on. She could breathe easier around him. Whatever came next, she could manage as long as she had him in her corner. She felt powerful, truly powerful.

Cole's growl grew louder until he pulled his

hands from her hair and lifted her easily off the couch. He didn't break the kiss as he crossed through his cabin. His steps didn't falter, and she didn't feel the slightest bit of nerves when he crossed the threshold into his room. His den.

He reached over his head and hauled his shirt off. She reached for him automatically. Like a magnet. She couldn't help herself. She needed to touch him.

She traced her fingers over each knuckle. Love and Hate were tattooed on his hands, and she understood that significance. They went together for a man like Cole. Hate replaced love, and the reminder stood out on his skin.

Up and up, over birds and flowers and geometric shapes and dot work and a whole host of other patterns adorning his skin. Over his shoulders. Across his collarbones. Down to his chest. "I love these," she said after her inspection.

With a soft growl, he reached for her. He undressed her slowly. Each inch of exposed skin was met with a kiss or nibble. Heat spread from his hands and mouth, warming her steadily until she was softly simmering in desire. Then, and only then, did he moved his hands to his jeans and kick them off his legs.

He settled on the bed next to her and drew her

into his lap. More kisses dotted her skin, a hand in her hair tilting her head one way or the other. "I like your shoes next to mine."

Rylee nearly melted. The words were silly, but the feeling behind them was big and important. She fit in his life. She had a place in his home.

His erection pressed between her soaked folds. Cole shuddered, and his fingers dug into her hips. The bite of his grip was nothing compared to the jolt of pleasure when he rocked his hips and hit her where she was most sensitive.

"You suck at predicting the future. I won't run from you," she said into his neck. "Will you believe that?"

She rolled her hips, and he groaned. "Fuck, Rylee. I'll believe anything you say if you do that again."

So she did. "We'll see where this goes? You won't drive me away?" Because he felt important, too.

A soft growl rattled in his chest. He pulled her hand over his heart. "I don't think I could if I tried. I wouldn't live long. My bear would eat me alive."

He flipped her to her back, then pulled away just as quickly. Hurt and worry drew his brows together. "Shit, sorry."

He moved to turn them back over, but she rose up on her elbows instead. Perfect, caring man wanted her as comfortable as possible. "I want to try it like this." Heck, she wanted to try it every way possible as long as it was with him.

His eyes grew to a sexy gold. And hungry. He devoured every inch of her with a single sweep of his gaze. Then his nostrils flared and a wicked grin lifted his lips. "You smell so fucking hot for me. Is that true, little bit? Do you want me to touch you?"

He eased a hand between her legs and slid a finger inside her. She couldn't help but arch into the touch. A tiny moan dripped from her lips when he pressed his palm against her clit. He drew back, and a second finger joined the first.

"Yes," she moaned.

He eased over her, holding himself up on his elbows. He brushed her hair from her face and kissed her cheeks, her nose, her neck, her lips.

The head of his cock brushed against her. She tensed, he swept his eyes to hers, and she relaxed. There wasn't any other outcome under those glowing orbs.

Rylee trailed her hands up his flexed arms and over his tight shoulders. She dug her hands into his hair to pulled him down for another kiss. Slow, again, simply tasting each other.

Then Cole rolled his hips, steadily pushing inside

her. Her breath hollowed her stomach. Fire burned through her veins, ignited her limbs, and coiled in her core.

Cole buried his face in the crook of her neck. "No fear," she murmured. "Just wildflowers."

"I smell like wildflowers?" she asked, taken aback.

He pulled away from her enough to give her a smirk. His abs flexed as he drove deeper into her, drawing another moan from her. "You smell like the sexiest flowers in existence."

He sipped at her lips on the final word and devoured the increasing gasps and sighs he bubbled to the surface. He pumped into her harder, faster, until she writhed under him. There was no room for panic or fear when she chased pleasure. That thick, hot feeling boiled just under her skin, ready to erupt.

His control slipped, then broke entirely. Gold flashed even hotter and hungrier in his eyes. He stroked into her faster than before. Rougher. So dang good.

A growl rattled in his chest, surging at the top of each thrust. Cole wrapped an arm under her hips, hauling her closer and tangling them together. One roll, a second, and he bumped her clit. Her breath heaved in her lungs and her thighs tightened around his body. And his growl deepened even more, vibrating through her and shaking loose the last bit of pleasure to rain down all around her.

"Cole!" she moaned, a pulsing orgasm ripping through her. Teeth clamped down on her skin, hard but not hard enough to break, and Cole's growl turned to a groan of pleasure.

He slowed, breathing just as hard as her pants. He pushed himself to his elbows again and the gold slowly faded from his eyes. Feeling as drunk on him as she had that morning, she pressed her lips to his collarbone. "Cole?"

"Hmm?" He rolled to his back and pulled her across his chest.

She trailed her fingers over the tattoos above his heart. Wildflowers. She wanted to believe it was fate of some sort, even if every ounce of her education rejected the idea. The romantic uncurling from the dark, neglected corner of her mind liked that he said she smelled like wildflowers and he had them permanently on his skin.

"I like my shoes next to yours, too."

CHAPTER 19

Awareness slowly washed over Cole. He was in his bed, with a gorgeous woman curled against him. Like the night before—two nights in his den, now—she slept in his shirt. He buried his face in Rylee's hair. Sleepy wildflowers filled his nose.

His bear was quiet. No snarling, no urging him to get up and find a fight. Just... content.

Rylee's glasses sat on the nightstand like they belonged. Maybe they did. Maybe his bear was right. Maybe she wouldn't leave and maybe she was fated to be his mate.

There was still too much uncertainty for him to be truly comfortable. She could get sick of his shit and want to leave. He could hurt her somehow. That seemed about a thousand percent certain of happening. But he would honor the promise she forced from his lips. They would try.

The sound of gravel crunching under tires jerked his attention out of bed. One vehicle wouldn't be alarming, but there were at least three. The clan didn't have any plans the previous night, so it wasn't a group returning home. With morning light just breaking over the territory, it was too early for visitors.

He was out of bed and tugging on his jeans before Rylee could mutter any objections. He drew a shirt over his head as he padded through his living room. Rylee was awake now, softly calling his name.

He opened his front door to see the other cabins in the clearing doing the same. Judah pushed open the door to his cruiser, and others followed from their own cars. All of the officers were focused entirely on him.

Whatever the fuck was up, it didn't bode well for him.

Callum was already moving across the center when Judah and one of his deputies took their first step to his porch.

Cole leaned against one of the wood columns. "You here to bring me breakfast, Judah? Can't see why you'd be here so early otherwise."

Judah made a face. "My hands are tied. You know I wouldn't do this otherwise."

"Do what? What's going on?" Callum demanded, pushing past Judah to take a stand with Cole.

Rylee took that moment to appear. She'd thrown on jeans and still wore his shirt, but her hair was as messy as when she woke. Fear and anxiety didn't just waft off her. It rose in thick clouds that set his bear on murderous edge.

Judah took one look in her direction and Cole let out a low growl. So much for a quiet bear. The monster in him wanted out. It needed to get between Rylee and every single male that'd come to his den.

"Cole Strathorn, you're going to need to come with me." Judah grasped his cuffs. "You're under arrest for the murder of human Maxwell Baker. You have the right to remain silent. Anything you say can and may be used against you."

"Cole, I order you not to lose your shit," Callum hissed. "We'll get this cleared up." A wave of power washed over him and grabbed hold of his bear.

Don't lose his shit? Fucking hilarious. He pushed against grasp Callum had over him. Pushed and shoved at it. Fuck his brother. Fuck his alpha. They weren't going to pin a murder on him.

"That's bullshit!" Cole spat. "I haven't gone near those camps since the last fire."

"When? When did this happen? He was with me all night!" Rylee yelled. Judah and Callum both winced at the sudden noise piercing their sensitive ears. Cole was too numb to care.

"Judah!" Callum shouted over the noise of Rylee still screaming her head off about the injustice of it all and the others of the Strathorn clan backing her up. "What happened?"

Judah continued with the spiel and snapped the silver cuffs around his wrists. Cole could feel his bear rampaging in his head, but there was nothing the beast could do. Silver locked him inside even better than Cole ever managed. The psychopath was roaring and demanding blood and Cole couldn't fault him one bit, especially when he caught sight of a new vehicle pulling up behind the police cruisers.

Major Assface Delano strode forward like he owned the place, flanked by men with huge weapons slung across their chests. He showed all the swagger of a man scared of his surroundings but backed up by a high caliber weapon. Coward couldn't even face the clan himself. He sent Judah to do the work and had a backup squad waiting in his truck.

A snarl ripped out of Cole. Maybe it was good he

was cuffed. He wouldn't be able to hold himself back. He wanted to tear the man to pieces.

He was going to burn the cabin down and rebuild if he ever got free. The man's boots on his porch were tainting his home.

Delano smirked like he'd won. He leaned close enough to almost press his nose against Cole's. *Just a little closer, asshole,* Cole begged. *I'll rip your fucking throat out.*

Delano spoke over Judah's attempt at a calm recitation of rights. "Your boy has a problem with humans, doesn't he? Just can't stand 'em in his territory. We got a dead college kid all mauled up and I know from personal experience how this one lashes out."

White fury was the only thing that kept Cole's mouth shut. He wouldn't give Delano the satisfaction of seeing him break. Judah could drive him down to the police department, lawyers would be called, and Delano's trick would fizzle into nothing. He couldn't have done shit when Rylee was with him all night.

And then, when the man least expected it, he'd have what little brain he possessed removed from his body.

"I'll be taking him now," Delano announced with

the smugness of a man who didn't know he was dead.

Cole stiffened. "Fuck that. No," he snarled.

Delano's eyes were full of hate when he nodded to his goons to grab hold of a shoulder each. "Outside your territory is outside your jurisdiction. I got the local PD asking for my help. Seems I'm not the only one who doesn't trust these small town wannabes not to let you go around the corner. To keep the civilians safe, you're coming with me."

Rylee pushed herself between men that towered over her. Anger replaced the fear, and her eyes flashed dangerously. "You can't do this!"

Delano puffed out his chest in a comical attempt at masculinity. He leaned down and nearly pressed his nose to Rylee. That move drew a growl from Cole, and Delano spared him a glance before turning his vicious gaze back on his woman. "You should have gone back to Nevada like you were told."

CHAPTER 20

Rylee paced from one end of the room to the other, then spun on her heel and marched back the other direction. The skin of her hands felt irritated with each turn and twist of her fingers, but she couldn't stop wringing them.

"Rylee, *stop*," Leah begged from her spot on the couch. She rubbed at her nose, mirroring the gesture from nearly every other Strathorn clan member in the room. "You're stinking up the place and making me want to shift."

Rylee gave her a withering look. Not even the silver of Leah's eyes could contain her agitation and anger. "Good! Do that, and get Cole back!"

"It's not that easy," Callum rumbled. He scrubbed a hand over his face and pushed away from the wall he leaned against to peek outside the windows. There was no movement.

They were waiting impatiently for Olivia to arrive. She'd gathered up a lawyer from inside the town and drove straight to the edge of enclave territory the second she heard one of her citizens had been detained.

Rylee resumed her pacing. A sharp growl made her scurry to find a seat, but even then she couldn't keep still. She drummed her fingers on the arm of the chair and wallowed in the memory of that morning.

It was another hour of waiting before the bear shifters perked to attention. Rylee held her breath until she heard a car approaching. She dug her fingers into her pants to keep from jumping up and pressing her face to the nearest window.

Olivia had barely entered the cabin when she held up a hand demanding silence to the questions bombarding her. "Sit, all of you. And keep your mouths shut. I don't want to repeat myself."

With enough grumbling to register on the Richter scale, the Strathorn clan crammed themselves into seats on the couch and the floor. Satisfied, Olivia proceeded with her report. "It's a precarious situation. The scene of the crime was outside of our territory, which would put Cole under county jurisdiction. They say they have his blood as evidence. But the local cops claim they don't have a facility capable of holding one superhuman, and they requested aid from the military."

"One guess who pressured that to happen," Leah muttered.

Olivia nodded tersely. "As for Delano, his spokesperson cited the obscure laws from the second World War allowing the detention of citizens by military forces. Same line they fed us when they first arrived. That's where we're at. Calls have been made up the chain."

Fuck. Shit. Damn. Rylee didn't even like to curse but there weren't any other words that fit the situation. Major Brant Delano had utter control of her world. He'd made his complaints and helped Peter usurp her position for research. And when she thought she'd found her place with Cole, he took that from her, too.

Her heart grew heavy under the weight of her pain. She couldn't hope to overcome Delano and all his resources. She should just walk away and resume her quiet, unassuming life and forget everything about Bearden.

And the woman she'd been between Peter's

attack and meeting Cole would have done just that. Bearden, and Cole in particular, had changed her. She couldn't walk away from him. She couldn't let him suffer whatever Delano had planned for him.

"Oh. Oh my god!" She whirled around to the room full of bears in various stages of anger and sullen fury. She could kick herself for not thinking of it sooner. She'd been too twisted up in knots to take the time to make the connection. "I think I know what he's planning!"

The screen door slapped shut and her feet thumped down the steps of Callum's porch before anyone jumped after her. She raced across the clearing and back into Cole's cabin. Her laptop. She'd grabbed it and a few other things from her room at the bed and breakfast after her dismissal from the lab yesterday. And if she wasn't mistaken, her backup of documents was waiting in the bottom of her bag.

She felt a chill recalling the plans laid out. She didn't think they'd be used, but she could already see how they were falling into place. Delano and Peter both hated the enclave's unnatural residents. Cole's alleged murder of a human would be the justification to eradicate the entire enclave.

She shot back out of Cole's cabin and met up

with a jogging and surly Nolan on her way back to Callum's. Breath heaving in her lungs, she ripped open her bag and dug out the USB drive and laptop.

"This," she panted. "This is what is being planned. Delano wants to destroy this place."

She shook her hair back from her face and adjusted her glasses. A few quick clicks on the keyboard brought up the document she needed. She was so keyed up she didn't even feel a trace of nerves with the large men crowding and jostling for position behind her.

She read through the document again, predicting what they were reading by the grunts and ground teeth. Justification for provocation. Nonessential and civilian evacuation. Communication jamming and power cutting. Infiltration. Eradication.

"You're just now bringing this to our attention?" Callum asked in a low, dangerous voice.

Rylee twisted and found faces in various stages of anger staring back at her. Olivia appeared to be the only one not wishing to rip her open at that moment, so she switched her attention back to Callum.

He was alpha to the entire clan and brother to the man that'd been taken. She could only imagine the difficult position he was in. Wanting to protect all of his people. Wanting to save his brother. What was the right move when the choice to save one might mean destruction for the others? And when that one was his own flesh and blood?

"I didn't think it would come to this," she murmured. "I thought it was the same sort of planning that's done for everything. Alien invasions? Running the country from planes after a nuclear attack? Why do you think the president and vice president aren't allowed to travel on the same planes? Because plans for some devastating tragedy are in a binder somewhere."

She squared her shoulders and met Callum's eyes. "You came out of nowhere. An entire town where people are *actual* storied creatures from horror movies. I know you're not a threat. I assume most people will arrive at that same conclusion. But you have to admit that it's a shock. And people are reassured when plans are in place to keep them safe." She pointed to the screen. "These plans aren't bad. It's the manufacturing evidence to kick start them that's evil. I think that's what Delano has done."

While she watched, the wifi signal vanished. She surged to her feet and patted down her pockets, searching for her cell. "Phones. Phones! Check your signals. Now!"

She snatched her phone off the coffee table where she'd left it. No signal bars were available, but she tried connecting a call anyway. Dead air answered her.

Slowly, she pulled the phone from her ear and pointed to one of the steps. "If this isn't a fluke, water and power will be next." Her eyes searched for Olivia. "Did you see any other camps?"

Olivia made a face. "We weren't allowed close enough."

"Fuck!" The word exploded from Callum's mouth. His words were tight. "We need to get word out and stop this madness before it begins."

"Who can we trust?" Sawyer demanded.

Leah cleared her throat, and all eyes turned to her. "That reporter is sitting in the civilian camps. The one that did the interview with Jamin? She didn't go running when he revealed us and she's been trying to get more of us on the record. She'd probably drown in her own drool at the chance to report on this."

"Good. Good." Olivia nodded. "Now we just need to pray she can be found if the roads are packed with people. If not, there has to be someone willing to publish that information. We need to be loud and get everyone's attention. I want the media reporting on this from coast to coast so the people above Delano can't ignore this. We will not die in silence."

Callum nodded and turned to Nolan. "Go to Gideon and the Bloodwings. We need to get that drive out of here."

"How? How will that help? They aren't going to let anyone cross the border."

"We have dragons," Leah said, as if that explained everything.

"Oh." Rylee's fingers shook as she copied the contents to her desktop. She'd seen enough disasters with lab work not backed up to let the only copy out of her sight. Done, she ejected the drive and handed it over, still not quite believing an explanation of dragons. Nolan was out the door as soon as his hand closed around the plastic case.

The plan of being loud was a good start, but it wouldn't be enough. Delano could pass materials off to start a hidden war using her research. A tip-off to a militia here, a few rousing speeches to the wrong sort of folk there, and hatred could spread like wildfire. She couldn't let them have tools to aid in their destruction.

She took a deep breath and made her announcement. "I need to get inside Delano's camp."

Everyone looked at her like she'd grown a second head. She thought it just as likely.

"My home facility already has my notes and preliminary findings. Any samples I collected were to be kept inside the enclave or at a mobile lab inside Delano's camp, per the agreement allowing me here. Those samples need to be destroyed. I won't have them used for nefarious purposes." With only one way they could have gotten Cole's blood, her work was already being used to harm.

Leah gave her a long, considering look while objections rose up all around them. Arguments were made for her leaving—getting out of danger, being another voice to support their claims—or staying— no telling what's planned inside that camp, Delano's monstrous nature. She kept silent through them all. They could argue till they were blue in the face. She was still going to find a way to destroy any samples Delano and Peter stole.

Leah raised her voice to be heard above all the others. There was no friendliness in her silver eyes. "Can you do it?"

"There is no other option. I'm the only human that's been allowed through. Anyone else will be recognized as an enclave resident and not allowed one inch across the border."

Leah looked like she wanted to say more. Rylee could hear the words. The other woman meant if she could keep herself together in the situation. Rylee didn't care. Her words still stood regardless of interpretation.

After a beat, Leah nodded. "I have something for you to give Cole if you can manage. Tell him we're coming for him."

"And what happens then?" Rylee asked.

She expected Leah or Callum to answer, but it was Olivia who stepped forward. "Then everyone able to defend their homes will prepare to fight." Her grin showed too many teeth. "You're not the only one with contingency plans, human."

CHAPTER 21

The camp had grown overnight. Cole didn't need his eyes to be certain. More voices and more smells. They couldn't hide those from him with a blindfold.

Canvas rustled and parted. He could sense where the air thickened against the tent walls feet from where he stood. Hearts beat in four corners. The tang of unease was sharp enough to taste.

The simple handcuffs from Judah were changed to thick shackles around his wrists and ankles. Silver, still. He wanted to laugh. The thickness of the metal didn't matter. It was the silver that did the trick. Chains probably made the puny humans feel safer from the beast at the top of the fucking food chain.

"String him up," Delano ordered with a touch of glee in his voice.

That wasn't good. Nor was the sudden jerking of his arms overhead. Chains pulled at him, links clanking together and raising his hands inch by inch. Cole felt the stretch in his muscles. Then he rose up on his toes.

"That's good. Tie him off and leave us," Delano commanded again.

Another clanking, another rustle of canvas, and the nearest heartbeats reduced down to one.

Cole traced that sound as it circled him, tilting his head from side to side for maximum effect. Delano had him strung up like a hunted deer, but he wasn't about to submit. The man needed to know how easily he could be hunted. Would be, just as soon as he got free. Delano and that asshole Peter would be torn to pieces.

Delano's scent of body odor and used cigars sliced through the air a second before the blindfold was ripped away from Cole's face. He blinked at the sudden light, adjusting quickly.

Delano snatched his chin between his fingers and gave him a look worthy of any trader eyeballing a prospective horse. "Your murder comes at just the right time. Word came down that the blockade was to be eased around this hellhole. You and I both know that can't happen."

"You and I both know I didn't do shit. So why don't you let me go, pack up your toy soldiers, and leave," Cole growled.

Delano smirked. "We have your DNA all over the crime scene."

"What is this? You're so bored babysitting us you had to make your own police procedural?" He rolled his eyes to the canvas roof above him. Oh, Rylee. He should never have let her take samples from him. "Believe me. I wouldn't be stupid enough to leave my blood behind."

Delano ignored him and took out a cigar from a pocket. He stuffed one end between his lips and grinned. "You're going to admit what you did to that boy. And then we're going to make sure it never happens again."

"Well, that doesn't exactly sound legal." Cole shrugged as much as he could with his arms hauled over his head. "What are you getting out of all this? A little revenge because I kicked your ass? Let me loose, we'll go another round."

Delano threw a punch that hit him square in the jaw. Cole spat blood. He could feel his busted lip and cheek slowly knitting together. Too slow, thanks to the fucking silver. He glared at Delano. "At least you look prettier with the scars I gave you."

Delano's expression didn't change even the tiniest bit as he socked another punch into Cole's stomach. "I changed since that day, you know. Prone to anger, but that can be all down to this shit duty and the little asswipes under my command. But the red meat, that's new. Never liked it as much or as red as I do now."

The man unleashed a series of punishing blows, using Cole as a punching bag. Cole winced at a sharp crack. There went a rib.

Delano took a step back and wiped his brow. "I can handle the red meat. Beats swallowing my service weapon after turning into a freak."

Cole grinned wildly. Someone would be working to get him free. Callum, Rylee, probably even Olivia Gale. He just had to outlast Major Assface Delano. Easy to do, when he could take a beating. His bear welcomed the challenge. "Come a little closer and I'll see what I can manage."

COLE DIDN'T FIGHT when the soldiers threw him to the bare ground in another tent, another cage. He wheezed and winced when they secured the chains at his feet and wrists to deep stakes in the ground, just outside the bars so he couldn't pull them up.

He stared up at the canvas ceiling and focused on himself. He'd know if he pierced a lung, right? That might mean death, even for him. He had several bruised and broken ribs, but air still seemed to make it into his chest.

Fuck, but Delano could hit. The man probably had more bear in him than he realized. Rylee should find an excuse to draw his blood and see if he had the weird little ridges like Leah.

"You look like shit."

Cole blinked at the voice. He felt like shit. Hell, he should have smelled the other man in the tent. He wore enough cologne for the entire population of Bearden.

He directed his one good eye at the bearded, bedraggled man. He inhaled once, twice. Fur and desperation were light under the powerful cologne. Shifter of some kind. "You the traitor mapping the enclave border?"

"Traitor." The man's mouth twisted into a sour shape, like he hated the taste of the word. "That implies I had any choice in my actions. You can call me Jacob."

Cole hauled himself upright. Mistake. The tent spun worse than if he'd downed a keg of moonshine. *Heal, bear.*

The beast was utterly silent in his head. Huh. It only took being beaten within an inch of his life to get the bear to stop clawing at his mind.

Jacob was looking at him funny. Cole cut him off before he could say another word. "So, Jacob. What brings you to these parts? Cheap vacation?"

"You enclave shifters think you're so safe. You're worse off than those living on the outside. You're sitting ducks."

Cole eased back down to the ground. The tent wouldn't stop spinning and the madman's words were hurting his head. "Spoken like someone who doesn't have any fucking idea what enclave life is like. We have each other's backs. The Broken sacrificed themselves to make us safe."

"And yet, you're in hell with me. How soon until they find excuses to capture more?"

Cole grunted and tried to remember just how many vials of blood Rylee drew. That was a good indicator of how many murders could be framed. "We won't stand for that."

"How many of you are fighters? How many have families they want to protect? How many will choose family over enclave? You might think you're a nice, small town, but you're just a group of loosely affiliated packs. The first sign of shit hitting the fan will shatter everything you hold dear.

"You think this is the first enclave they've busted up? They have billionaires and soldiers in their ranks. Backwoods rednecks who sound like they're speaking a different language with accents so thick. These are the people that whisper in dark corners about hunting the most dangerous game. We're just intelligent animals to them. We're not even people in their eyes. I wonder how many of their ilk are in the ranks outside. New noises, new scents. They're beefing up for something big."

Maybe Jacob wasn't off his rocker. The camp had grown larger. Hunters had been a threat since the first dumbass with supernatural blood showed his ass. The enclaves were made to protect against those sorts of assholes.

But some had gone dark, even in recent years. Hunter attacks could be blamed in some cases, a need for relocation in others. If Jacob were to be believed, and Cole was unhappily conceding the point, they were sitting ducks and fish in a barrel and every other phrase that meant entirely fucked.

"Those animals want us dead," Jacob continued

with no emotion in his voice. "Don't hope for a rescue. I did, for a while. That was before they killed my entire pack."

Revulsion shivered down his spine. The loss was written on Jacob's face. The horror of it was ingrained in him. Losing every single person in his clan would kill him. A bond existed between them all, deeper than simply family. They were clan. They had each other's backs. They wouldn't abandon one of their own. Hell, he even counted on it. That resolve kept him from falsely admitting to a murder he didn't commit.

And that bond might be exploited to kill them all.

"What happened to you?" Cole asked, afraid he already knew the answer.

Jacob shrugged. "We made mistakes. Got careless. Brought attention to ourselves. Ring fights, that's what we did. Wounds healed too fast in front of too many eyes and the wrong sort of people saw."

His voice took on a dead tone, and he stared into nothing. "I got taken in the backwoods of Virginia after a fight. Drunk, high off the win, so I didn't see them coming. Spent a few days looking like you do now while they insisted that if I just behaved myself, they'd treat me well."

"Bet that went over well," Cole muttered. Bile

rose in his throat. The words were eerily similar to what Delano told him. Admit the truth, and he'd go easy on him. The beatings would stop if he would just admit what he'd done.

"Just made me want to fight even more." A smile ghosted Jacob's lips, then died. "But not in the way they wanted. They wanted brutal fights between animals. Dog fighting on steroids. Fox hunts. Knew a fox, once. They didn't want her fighting me. Wouldn't have been *entertaining*."

Something nudged at the back of Cole's mind. Foxes were rare. The only family he knew were the Holdens, and of those only Becca and Faith were still alive. Becca lived outside the enclave for a long while and she was cagey about her sudden return.

She'd say something, wouldn't she? Hell, she couldn't keep her mouth shut half the time. Jacob's fox couldn't be Becca.

"Two weeks, tops." Jacob sounded lost in a memory he'd rather forget. "That's how long it took them to force me to turn and fight in the ring. My wolf was going crazy by then. You know how it is. Can't stay to one shape too long or you start feeling that itch to shift. Can't stay cooped up in a cage without going a little insane. But there's only so much you can do when you're tossed in a cage and facing down the slavering jaws of a grizzly. So I fought.

"Then a new breed came in. They said they needed to know my abilities to assess the threat. Needed to know if I was born or if something happened to make me the way I was. They told me they wanted me to be their next super soldier. A smarter tracker. A glorified bloodhound to find more like me. And I refused."

"Good man," Cole muttered.

"I refused until the day they dragged me out of my cage, threw me to the ground, and forced me to watch them put a bullet in the head of my entire pack. For research and continued cooperation, I was later told."

Cole slammed the heel of his hand into the earth below him. "Fuck!"

"If you want my advice," Jacob continued coolly, "just give them what they want. They'll kill everyone anyway, but it'll save you some pain. And if they make us fight, rip out my throat when I give it to you."

Cole snarled. The faces of his clan wavered in his mind. Delano had plans that were unfolding while he sat useless in a cell with a broken wolf. He couldn't roll over and play dead. He wouldn't.

He settled into watching and waiting for an opportunity to escape. Food came and went, with guards posted inside the tent to make sure nothing of use was left behind. He wasn't even allowed a plastic spoon to shovel the slop into his mouth.

Sunlight overhead shifted from one side of the tent to the other, marking the time gone by. Hours passed without word to or from his people. Hours of plans made and discarded for one reason or another.

The guards posted at each corner of the tent outside did their jobs well. They hardly moved and didn't speak a word to anyone. He could almost forget they were there, which was the point. If he forgot they existed, he could be surprised by them if he somehow ditched the shackles on his wrists and ankles and chewed through the thick bars of the cage.

Fuck, fuck, fuck. And anyway bear was still silent.

Late afternoon arrived with no contact to the outside world when noises he didn't recognize as significant jerked Jacob to his feet. His cellmate's eyes went wide with fear and the scent of it overrode the cologne he was made to wear to hide his otherness. "Up. Up!"

Cole shook his head. If they wanted him on his feet, they could drag him upright.

"At ease, men," Delano stated on the other side of the tent opening.

Cole's pulse thudded in his head as Rylee walked through the tent flaps. Delano ducked inside on her heels, but it was the small woman that held Cole's attention.

Everything about her was tense. Her shoulders, her eyes, her jaw. She even walked like she was connected to taut lines above her.

But her smell. Holy hell, she smelled nervous enough to make him strain at his cuffs and want to fight. Even his bear rumbled in his head, making the first sound since Delano beat the beast into silence.

"Don't get too close," Delano ordered.

Rylee ignored him and stepped up to the bars of the cage. Her eyes flicked down to the ground in front of her, summoning him.

Cole pushed to his feet and took cautious steps forward. Delano stiffened behind her.

His head swam. Fuck, he'd taken too many blows in too short a time. He needed more rest than a single afternoon. He needed to shift.

He wasn't too proud to grab hold of the bars to

keep himself upright. "What are you doing here?" he asked her.

Rylee covered his hands with hers. Something rough poked between his fingers. He jerked, placing his hand over hers, and a tiny package crushed against his palm.

"I'm ready." She switched her attention to Delano. "This is him."

Delano cleared his throat and spat on the ground. She didn't even flinch. "You sure?"

Rylee nodded. "I heard him get up in the middle of the night. Curious, I followed him out of the Strathorn clearing and past guards on both sides of the barrier. I watched him wait for a human to come to the edge of the camp. He hunted like an animal and he slaughtered like one, too."

Cole felt every single kick and punch Delano gave him all over again. Only this time, they came from a woman he thought he could love.

Lies. So many lies. She stank of them. How no one else could tell, he didn't know.

But maybe that was the point. Maybe they didn't care. Her career was over. That rang loudly in his head, right after repeating her lies. Maybe no one cared because they were happy to believe her false words and use him as a scapegoat. Maybe she was happy to lie if it restored her reputation.

"What are you doing?" he growled. His bear sent him images of slapping the ground and roaring for her submission. She owed him answers for her lies.

She barely acknowledged him, eyes dipping to where their hands met before pulling away from him. She turned to Delano and lifted her chin. "Is that all you need from me?"

Delano bowed slightly and gestured to the tent flap. "That's everything. Let's get you set up for the night before you head back home." He waited until Rylee left before shooting Cole a triumphant grin. "You're a dead man. You, and the rest of your freak town," he hissed before stalking back outside.

Cole tightened his fist around whatever Rylee passed him. He shuffled to a bucket in the corner. At least Delano's men provided that much. He used the fumbling of his button and zipper to hide opening the tiny parcel.

The note had two words. *We're coming.*

Tucked inside was a tiny set of lock picks, straight out of Leah's collection.

Jacob's words roared to life with his bear. The beast raked his brain with sharp claws and visions of death. Jacob's pack was destroyed to gain his cooperation. Delano stood poised to pull the trigger against the entirety of Bearden, and he had Rylee in his camp for the first shot.

His bear didn't care why she lied or made the stupid decision to enter the camp. He only wanted to save her from death.

He had to get out of the cage before everyone he cared about was killed.

CHAPTER 22

R ylee's stomach twisted and turned. Cole looked awful. More than awful. More than terrible. She didn't even know how to describe the violence written across his skin.

He should have healed. Why hadn't he healed? How long ago were his injuries taken and why was he nearly purple with all those bruises?

And who, exactly, was the other man in the second cell?

She bit her tongue to keep herself from screaming at the top of her lungs how fucked up everything around her truly appeared. She couldn't help anyone if she broke down. Survival was the game now. She'd passed on Leah's message and lock picking tools. She needed to wait for her chance to escape, hopefully after she was able to destroy the samples stolen from her lab.

Rylee lifted her chin regally and faced Delano. "Is that everything you need from me?" she asked again.

Delano spoke around his cigar. "Like I said, we'll get you set up for the night. We have training exercises planned and I can't spare anyone to take you to the airport."

Training exercises. Rylee wanted to spit at his feet and call him a liar. The surrounding preparation wasn't for training. Everyone was too keyed up. They were going into battle with more soldiers than she'd seen when she first arrived in Montana.

She doubted Delano even waited for clearance on his falsified provocation, of which she now played a role with her witness statement intended to get her back inside the camp, but he'd certainly received additional troops from somewhere. He was prepared to go in without orders and slaughter innocent lives. No doubt he a plan to justify that, too.

He was even more dangerous than she imagined.

With a sarcastic bow and wave of his hand, Delano escorted her through the camp.

She memorized the layout and even marked off what appeared to be a bus in the center of the camp. Power was diverted to several large areas, likely for the open-walled mess tent and a closed command station. But the hard walls and huge wheels of the vehicle meant it likely served as a mobile lab and held the refrigerated samples she needed to destroy.

Three rows down and one over, Delano ushered her inside a small tent and left a trio of guards outside with strict orders to keep her from leaving. Rylee entered without a word. She expected to be detained. It was part of the plan, even. She played her part and now she waited.

And waited.

And waited.

She paced the few feet allotted to her, turned, and paced in the other direction. She drummed her fingers on her thighs and tried to urge herself to patience. One minute slipped into ten, then into an hour.

How long would it take for a dragon to find and convince a reporter that an entire town was about to be murdered? What noise needed to be made before some government or military official made a phone call to stop the madness? And what happened to Bearden in the time it took for someone's attention to be snagged?

The late afternoon dragged on. The bag she brought to sell her story of leaving Bearden was brought to her, no doubt thoroughly searched. Her laptop was missing, along with her phone, not that either would do her good if Delano had communication blocked. The guards outside her tent even passed her a small lantern for the evening before leaving her alone once again.

Rylee stopped her pacing and laid down on the cot. She didn't know how long she stared at the canvas ceiling and willed something to happen when a monstrous, prehistoric roar filled her ears.

Shouts followed, then the slapping of feet on the packed ground.

When she peeked out of the tent, the guards posted there pointed and raised their weapons to the giant beast in the sky. She followed their gaze and got her first glimpse of a dragon hovering above the camp. Deep scarlet scales glittered in the dying light. Bullets ricocheted off the dragon's underbelly and only served to make him angry. Swift swoops of his wings twisted him this way and that, and another roar was accompanied by a jet of fire above the camp.

That had to be her signal. There was no other reason a dragon would appear when she desperately needed one.

Rylee shot out of the tent and straight toward the

bus in the center of the camp. Her guards barely gave her a second glance, focused instead on the sky. Two more dragons appeared out of thin air, then a fourth. They danced above the camp, roaring and spitting fire above the heads of the soldiers left behind.

Too many were gone, she noted as she ran. Only the barest of guards remained. A lump grew in her throat. Delano was already making his move on Bearden. Maybe the dragons would be distraction enough to turn him back toward the camp and away from the innocent lives in the enclave.

Rylee paused across from the mobile lab. Another roar directly above her forced her to clap her hands over her ears. She glanced skyward and found a dragon hovering overhead. Nerves bubbled to life, but the flame she expected to burn her alive never came. No flames touched the ground, in fact. The dragons weren't out for blood. Yet.

Filled with a new respect, Rylee snapped her attention back to the mobile lab and ran for the door. The dragons were creating a loud, fiery show, and she needed to finish her mission and get out.

She hated what she was about to do, but she couldn't let any of the samples she collected fall into anyone's hands but her own. Not when she didn't know who she could trust, or where they would end up. If she was right and Delano was on some mad witch hunt to end supernatural lives, her work could be used to help perfect methods of slaughter. He might still have access to her reported findings, but he'd need to acquire more samples to continue any study into harm. She needed to make his goal as difficult as possible.

She tore open the fridge, then snapped open the tops of sealed containers. Blood she'd been trusted to draw dribbled onto the floor, one tube after another. Hair and cheek swabs followed, all in one giant mess.

She searched through the cabinets until she found bottles of peroxide and alcohol. Those, too, were dumped over the puddle of blood. She didn't know if she could make the whole lab go up in smoke, but the samples would still be ruined if she failed.

The door flung open and heavy steps thumped up the three stairs to the inside. Rylee froze, the bottle of alcohol in hand. She knew who those footfalls belonged to even before she turned around.

Peter approached slowly, a sick grin on his face and his hands raised to convey some sense of calm.

"I told Brant to keep a better eye on you. There was no chance you'd flip so easily."

Her mind flashed back to that awful night. He approached her then the same way. His outstretched hands were meant to calm—and to catch. The slimy smile on his face was meant to entice but only elicited fear. Pure terror dumped into her veins and kept her frozen in panic as he approached.

Slowly. Steadily. Like a snake slithering near to its prey.

He couldn't be allowed to touch her again. She'd rather die than let his fingers bruise her skin. He did enough damage to shake her to her core. Just as she was breaking through the choppy waves and sucking in a fresh breath, he threatened to drag her under again.

"By all means, keep destroying those. We have more stashed away. You barely touched the surface of what we already know." He looked thoughtful. "The concentration of blood cells in the vampire's sample was new, though. We're hoping to snag one on this trip."

This trip? Her panic was crushed by a wave of queasiness. This wasn't the first time they'd hunted supernaturals. She should have known the other man in Cole's tent wasn't just someone who broke some rules.

"What are you going to do to him?"

"The bear?" Peter shrugged. "Depends on how cooperative he is. If he doesn't listen, he might just be sold off for ring fights. Our wolf needed to be broken, but now he's a good dog. He's been used to map the entire enclave. Prior to this, pain tolerance and advanced healing were studied. We know what we're dealing with inside the barrier."

"Why are you telling me this? You're admitting to torturing someone." She already knew the answer, but Peter was a talker. If she could keep him distracted, maybe she could find a way around him. There was an exit at the back, but the spilled blood and chemical mixture was a fall hazard she couldn't risk in the precious seconds she had before he was on her. No, the best choice was the front of the trailer and a door without an emergency latch to break open.

Failure was not an option. She couldn't leave Cole or that other shifter to whatever fate waited for them at Delano's hands or Peter's research. Neither deserved to be hurt or used. She'd burn the entire camp to the ground before she let them destroy any more innocent lives. The entire population of

Bearden needed protecting. They didn't deserve death simply for being different.

"Because you're not getting out of this." He tucked a piece of hair behind her ear and lightly brushed his knuckles over her jaw. "We had some good times back in school, didn't we? You'd be a good fit for my team."

She recoiled away from his touch. Air rushed in and out of her lungs. Too fast. She focused on slowing her breathing. She didn't need to hyperventilate or lose herself in a full-blown panic attack. Clawing to keep her sanity, she took a step back. "Don't touch me," she hissed.

Peter smirked. "I forgot you like to put up a fight. Brant says we might find a use for you when we bring in the other animals. That's what you like now, isn't it? Fucking the beasts?"

Another roar shook the mobile lab. Peter jerked his attention skyward, even though he couldn't see anything through the ceiling.

Rylee took her chance. Something terrible was taking place in Bearden and she couldn't let Peter stand in her way of aiding even one person.

She snatched up the nearest microscope, wrapping both hands around the neck. Peter let his attention fall back to her just as she raised the base and slammed it into his cheek with a sickening crunch. Years of fear and anxiety and anger and questions of why her and what she could have done to prevent it went into the blow. And when the microscope fell from her hands, a fraction of the weight he tied around her neck fell with it.

Peter crumpled to the ground with a thud and she jumped over his body. She didn't glance behind her. She couldn't, no matter how much she wanted to witness his pain and suffering. Her escape was more important than her satisfaction.

CHAPTER 23

Cole paced the cage in his mind, not wanting to drag the chains along with him and bring down the attention of the guards. Rylee told lies about him, but she also brought him a message from his clan. Did she truly mean to wash her hands of him and Bearden to save her reputation? Giving him the means of freeing himself might be her way of absolving herself of the lies.

"Who was that?" Jacob asked.

"No one," Cole answered.

Or had she simply decided the lies were the easiest way to get back into Delano's camp to pass him the lock picks? Cole didn't think she was capable of hurting anyone. Delano, though, was suited to causing pain, and she'd placed herself within his grasp.

An hour passed and Cole was no closer to figuring out the woman's motives. Nor was he any closer to freeing himself. Too much noise would alert the guards and he couldn't let the lock picks or note be found.

We're coming.

But when?

The first roar drew confusion from the guards. They poked their heads through the flap, quickly scanned Cole and Jacob's cages, then ducked right back outside.

Then the shouting began.

Cole grinned wildly. Delano and his bastards might have plans to capture Bearden, but they wouldn't find an easy fight. His people knew what it meant to be driven to survive. Their ancestors sacrificed themselves to make the safety of the enclaves. No one would give up their homes or lives without first painting their claws and fangs with blood, despite what Jacob predicted.

The ratcheting sound of gunfire dropped him to his ass. He dragged out the lock picks from the pocket of his jeans and tried to fit the first pick into the keyhole of a shackle on his wrist.

"What do you have there?" Jacob asked from across the tent. His chains clanked as he rose from his bed of dirt and crawled toward the bars.

"Gonna get us out of here," Cole muttered. He twisted his hands around and again tried to fit the pick to the keyhole. The silver shackles burned his already irritated skin and he grit his teeth against the rubbing, scuffing pain. He had no time for that.

"Fuck!" The pick snapped and fell uselessly to the ground.

He should have practiced more with Leah. But oh, no. He thought he was a big shot the one time he got the cuffs off his wrist and hadn't bothered with it since. He was paying for that mistake now.

Another roar sounded overhead. Both he and Jacob looked up, then back down to the other.

"Pass them here," Jacob insisted.

"I can get it," Cole grunted. He switched from trying to twist at his wrists to releasing his ankles. If he could do one, he could do the next and he didn't need to fight his limits to reach the keyhole on the shackles around his ankles.

"Before the dragons set this place on fire? Or before you break them all?"

Cole hesitated. Jacob was right. It was only a

matter of time before the fires above reached the ground.

But could he trust the man? He'd been held captive, beaten, and broken. He saw his entire pack murdered. He had every reason to hate the men outside their cages and zero reason to trust Cole. He could easily free himself and run or try to curry special favors by throwing Cole under the bus.

Rylee's presence in the camp decided for him. She had to know there was no safety with Delano in control. She was caught in Cole's den. She'd be lined up with the rest of his clan if Delano wanted to break him as he broke Jacob. He needed to guarantee she was safe and he couldn't do that stuck behind bars with only broken lock picks as a reminder of her.

Cole stuffed the pick in his hand back into the little packet and tossed it across the tent. It landed just outside of Jacob's cage and the wolf dove for it, straining to stretch his arm through the bars. His fingers brushed against the leather, then dragged it close enough to snatch up.

"Hurry," Cole urged, glancing toward the tent flap. Gunfire and shouting still sounded outside. Rylee would be in the middle of all that noise and activity.

"This will go faster if you stay quiet," Jacob muttered. He worked deftly. One solid twist on each ankle freed his legs. He changed picks and twisted his wrists until those shackles, too, clattered to the bare ground.

Jacob's eyes glowed gold as he twisted his wrists and rolled his shoulders.

"You're good with those," Cole said. He wanted to keep Jacob's attention. He'd be harder to leave behind if Jacob was in an active conversation.

"Didn't exactly lead a good life before it all went to shit." He knelt at the door to his cage and fumbled with two picks. He wiggled and nudged them together almost tenderly, and planted an ear close to the lock to listen while he worked.

Something inside clinked, and the door swung open. Jacob was on his feet and out of the cage fast enough that he blurred.

The tent flaps rustled and Rylee burst inside, cheeks red from exertion.

Cole's bear roared with relief at the sight of her. She was here. She was safe. Delano hadn't used her for target practice.

"We have to go—"

Jacob struck quickly, wrapping his hand around her throat and cutting her words off entirely. Her eyes went wide and rolled between him and the other shifter.

Cole rushed the bars of his cage. His hands slapped around the metal, shackles on his hands and feet clanking together with the motion. "Let her go!"

Jacob's hand tightened and Rylee wheezed. "She's with them."

"She's also the one that brought us the fucking picks. Let. Her. Go!" Locked away as he was, Cole still called on his bear to lace his words with power. It was a trickle, at best, nothing near the force he could manage when not bound by silver. He had no link to Jacob to compel him to listen. But it made his words serious.

Jacob's eyes flickered from the glowing gold of his wolf to the deep green of his human side. He blinked. And released Rylee.

Rylee sagged and drew in a shaky breath. She slunk away from Jacob, taking a place in the corner furthest from the man. Fear wafted off her and Cole moved down the cage to put himself in her eye line.

"Rylee. Rylee, listen to me. Jacob is not going to hurt you. He's going to get me out of here." Cole shot a dirty look toward Jacob. "Open the fucking cage!"

Jacob dropped to his knees and played with the

door, but Cole already put his attention back on Rylee. Her breath evened out and panic slowly subsided, but it didn't quite disappear. Under that acrid scent that made him want to wring Jacob's neck was something sharper and familiar. Blood and chemicals. She smelled like her lab.

"There," Jacob announced. The door banged open, and he hurried forward, poking and prodding at the shackles on Cole's wrists, then ankles.

Cole shoved Jacob aside as soon as he was free and crossed to Rylee in three long steps.

"I'm sorry. I'm sorry. I didn't want to betray you, but it was the only way I could get inside the camp. I had to destroy the samples, but even that was all for nothing because this isn't the first time your people have been hunted down and used for terrible things."

He cupped her cheeks and captured her lips in a rough kiss full of clashing tongues and teeth. He wanted to possess her, show her she belonged to him and with him. His bear rumbled in the back of his head and the noise spilled out of his chest. Contentment. That was what she gave him, even in the middle of a war zone. She was everything good in the world.

Immediately, the nerves that clouded the air

around her faded to nothing. She relaxed into him, hands skimming up his chest and wrapping around his neck.

There was only one reason why he felt the pain of her betrayal so deeply. She'd found her way past the walls around his heart and made a space for herself. She might not be ready to say the words, but he'd wait.

She was a flighty little thing that he had to coax into staying still, but she was his mate. He'd be a patient hunter, a patient lover, because he couldn't imagine living without her. He'd had a glimpse of a life with her and a life without, and he vastly preferred her with him.

All they needed to do was survive the night and kick out the damn occupying force intent on killing him and his people. Easy.

Jacob's agitation intruded and Cole pulled back from Rylee with a tiny bite of her lower lip.

Rylee rubbed her throat and eyed Jacob nervously. She tensed with his movement, following him as he stuffed the set of lock picks into a pocket and approached the entrance. "We need to go," she told Cole, still keeping her eyes on Jacob.

"You're right. You need to go." He glanced toward

Jacob, who nodded with unspoken agreement. They had business to finish that she didn't need to witness. "I need to get back to Bearden. I can help them. You should leave while you can. I'll come for you."

If he survived. The words were heavy even in their silence.

"No." She shook her head and repeated the word. "No. I'm staying with you."

"We don't have time for this," Jacob growled. He parted the tent flaps slightly and swiveled his head to check the sides. "We don't have anyone here. Those dragons are distractions. We need to go while they're still in the sky. If I'm to die today, I want it with blood on my teeth."

Cole's bear raked at his insides. Rylee needed to be safe, and what better way to guarantee that than by his side. There was no reasoning with the beast that anywhere else would be safer for her at that moment.

Gritting his teeth against the feeling of tearing himself in half, he found her big blue eyes on him. "There's going to be fighting and probably killing. Will you run if I say so?" Without hesitation, she nodded.

His bear roared and settled into the role of guardian. Rylee would survive and they would protect their people. She was their mate and deserved that protection. She belonged in Bearden and in their den.

Cole grabbed her wrist and whirled, shoving Jacob out of the tent.

The three ducked down and ran between rows of tents. Small groups of soldiers were still firing up at the dragons in the air. The beasts wheeled around and threw jets of flame over the heads of the little humans, but no fire burned on the ground.

Good, Cole thought briefly. No matter which way the night ended, the shifters couldn't be said to have burned a camp of innocent people. Dragons above without a ruined camp below would show restraint.

They neared a bus sitting in the middle of the camp and the door banged open. A man wobbled down the steps, tripping over his own feet and nearly missing the handrail to keep himself upright.

Cole snarled when he recognized Peter fucking Glasser. His face had seen better days. Pain and blood filled Peter's scent. Not enough. He needed more of both.

Peter held a hand to his head. "Rylee," he slurred, pointing a shaking finger at her.

Rylee stiffened right before Jacob again ghosted behind his target and grabbed Peter by the nape of his neck. Jacob's mouth twisted into a murderous look, with fangs slipping over his lips. "This one was there. He collected my pack after they were killed and cut them to pieces."

Cole nodded. As much as he wanted to be the one to do it for Rylee, Jacob had hold of the man. His capture, his kill.

Rylee sucked in a breath and turned into his chest as Jacob snapped Peter's neck.

A gun fired from behind them, then another. Two bullets struck the side of the bus above their heads. Cole pushed Rylee in front of him and around the bus with Jacob hot on their heels. It was a reminder of where they were and how dangerous it was to stop moving.

They made their way through the rest of the camp without much resistance. Most of the vehicles were gone. Vanished down the mountains and back toward human civilization or infiltrating enclave territory, Cole didn't know.

A boom sounded in the distance, followed by another. He turned at the noise. Smoke rose in the direction of Bearden. They were running out of time.

Jacob opened and closed his fists in agitation. "I can hotwire a truck."

"No time," Cole growled, already tugging his shirt over his head. It'd be quicker to run straight there and avoid any traps on the road. He kicked off his boots and stuffed his shirt into Rylee's hands. "You think you can hang on tight?"

She nodded, and he jerked his chin at Jacob. "Shift. We're running."

He'd barely thrown his jeans to Rylee when his bear shoved forward. The shift wasn't pretty or easy. His beast wanted blood and the quickest path to that was tearing through the puny human cage that held him.

Cole dropped to his knees, bones snapping and muscles tearing. Thick fur slid through his pores. His hands convulsed with their sudden growth, until long claws protruded from huge paws.

Shifted entirely, he turned his head to Rylee. Her eyes were wide behind her glasses and her lips parted as she stared at him. He scented the air, searching for any uncertainty in her. There was none. Excitement clung to her instead.

He huffed a breath, ruffling her hair, and her

smile broadened. He pressed his belly to the ground, and she climbed up his back.

With his mate's hands digging into his fur and a sleek grey wolf dancing at his side, Cole roared in the direction of Bearden.

He was coming.

CHAPTER 24

R ylee pressed her cheek against Cole's back and tightly squeezed her eyes shut. She focused her entire will on not throwing up. It'd go all over her, and Cole, and Cole and Jacob's clothes. She wanted neither the mess nor the embarrassment.

She knew shifters were fast. She'd watched them move around town in their human and animal forms. Nothing prepared her for the stomach-dropping reality on the back of one as he careened through the woods, dodging tree trunks and low branches like it was nothing.

She opened her eyes briefly. Mistake. Cole bunched his hind muscles and soared over a ditch. Every inch of her tightened and braced for a hard impact. The jolt, while less than what she imagined, still clattered her teeth together and a shocked squeak rushed from her lungs.

The wild ride slowed, then finally came to a stop. Cole pressed his belly to the ground but Rylee was already sliding from his back.

"Never again," she said weakly to the beasts shifting into very naked men. She adjusted her glasses and took a deep, calming breath. Anything to stop the rolling in her stomach. "Never doing that again."

Cole lifted her chin. The brief touch stopped her trembling and smoothed down her roughened nerves. "Find something in the distance, as far as you can see. Stare at that. It should help center you."

She found a tree in the distance and focused on it. Slowly, the queasiness in her stomach faded away.

Meanwhile, Cole separated his clothes and tossed the rest to Jacob. She was surprised to see most of his injuries had faded. More questions for later.

He tugged on his jeans and addressed the other man. "Barrier is down. I didn't feel it when we crossed."

Jacob nodded and stuffed his head through his shirt. "Makes sense. They send in a team with someone who can lead them through, separate the Broken to disconnect the barrier, and the rest of their forces can waltz in without a guide."

"That's what I'm afraid of. We have no way of knowing how many are swarming over the enclave." Cole rolled his shoulders and stared through the darkness. His eyes glowed gold with his bear. "You two stay here. I'll scout ahead."

"Cole—" Rylee began.

He ducked his head and pecked her on the lips. "Just for a moment. I'll be right back. Jacob will watch you."

COLE KEPT to the shadows of the trees, then to the alleys behind the buildings. The situation was worse than he imagined. Patrols roamed the streets, aided by lights mounted to helmets that were sure to catch the eye shine of any shifter in animal form.

Smoke poured out of the windows of homes and businesses, while soldiers waited at the exits to snare any shifter who wanted to avoid suffocation. Those were cuffed and thrown into big vehicles that waited in the middle of the street. Once full, the truck drove toward the other side of town. He didn't want to imagine why everyone in Bearden needed to be rounded up, but at least they weren't being slaughtered in the streets.

His bear itched with irritation to get back to their mate. Cole let the word sink into his bones as he padded on silent feet toward the place he left Rylee and Jacob. Mate was the right word. It slid across his mind and soothed his soul instead of scraping at him like the silver shackles on his skin.

With all the shit and rejection in his past, he never expected to find his fated mate. He never even expected to find someone to settle down with as a consolation prize. He was prepared to be the permanent bachelor of the clan, hiding his unease with quick smiles and jokes.

Then Rylee turned up, entirely human and ready to knock his world sideways. His bear chose the worst possible human to get involved with, and his heart followed suit. She'd been kicked down in a terrible way, but she'd also shown true bravery to walk back into Delano's camp to attempt freeing him.

The night held too many threats, but he and his bear were in full agreement. If they survived, he would mate Rylee properly. He almost pitied anyone that tried to stand in his way.

Noise in the distance interrupted his thoughts. He plastered himself to the side of a building and poked his head around. Two lights bounced with the steps of soldiers. Closer, he urged them. If they passed him, he could take them out without anyone else knowing.

Then Rylee shot across the street.

The soldiers both rushed to raise their weapons. "Don't move!"

Horror struck, he watched as Rylee slowed and turned, hands raised.

There was a flash of movement behind the pair of soldiers. Jacob struck one, then the other with a thick branch.

Cole shot out from the building before the soldiers hit the ground. "Where the hell were you?" he hissed at Jacob. "Why was she running right in front of them?"

"I was where I needed to be to take them down," Jacob said.

Cole shoved at Jacob's chest, forcing the man to stagger back a step. "She is not to be used as bait," he snarled.

"Cole, it was my idea!" Rylee tugged at his arm and he rounded on her.

"They could have shot you!"

"But they didn't. Jacob did what you asked and watched over me. They would have found us otherwise. And look, he didn't even kill them. That will look better for us in the long run."

"We couldn't stay where we were left. Too many of them crawling around," Jacob added softly.

Cole shook his head and let go of a tight breath. "Secure them. We need to get them out of the street before anyone else comes this way."

Cole threw one soldier over his shoulder while Jacob manhandled the other into place. They trotted into an alley and tossed both men into a dumpster.

"Get out of our town!"

The whispered shout came from a row of homes at the other end of the alley. Cole hurried to the corner of the building. Rylee poked her head around the corner after shoving him to the side and making room for herself under his arm.

Cole resisted the urge to pass a hand over his face. For a woman so wound up with anxiety, she was going to send him into a panic attack simply trying to keep her safe.

He peered over her head and saw three elderly

ladies beating a pair of soldiers with their large purses. One of the men attempted to grab the largest woman, but the one to her left made a fist and brought it down on his head. The second man was similarly subdued, then promptly kicked in the ribs.

"Cole Strathorn, is that you peeking around the corner? Is that doctor with you?"

"You seem to have everything in hand, Old Miss. Didn't want to take away your agency."

"My agency." Old Miss snorted. "Boy, get over here and bring your doctor. We have a way down into the tunnels. She shouldn't be roaming the streets tonight. Put her with the children before she hurts herself."

Rylee made an offended noise. Cole shook his head. He should have expected the town's crotchety gossips, unaffectionately known as the Old Maids, to run a resistance force.

The trio jogged across the street and followed the Old Maids between two houses. Old Miss flung open wooden doors to a basement, then stood back. She gave him a wink and a quick slap on the ass. "Downstairs with you. We've rounded up those we could and stuck them with the vampires. Victor will get you to the real fighting."

Feeling like they were running from one scene of

madness to the next without any consideration, Cole led Rylee and Jacob into the basement. From there, it was clear where to go. The Old Maids dropped the outer doors closed just as they crossed the threshold of a door leading to the tunnels below Bearden.

Rylee's second journey into the lower city was wilder than before. The nighttime residents were out in full force, but a large number of shifters were underground, too. The spider web of connections to the topside were filled with people moving toward the inner sanctum of the vampires.

The room opened on a crowded, noisy space. Some parents clutched their crying and confused children, while others stared into the distance with hardened jaws and angry expressions. It seemed the Old Maids had done a fair job in smuggling people out from under the noses of the soldiers.

But there were still too many missing, Cole thought as he glanced around. The room couldn't hold everyone, certainly. But he'd seen too many loaded up into trucks and hauled elsewhere. He could only hope that many more were able to prepare to fight between the time he was taken to the moment the first of Delano's troops crossed the enclave border.

If it came down to the enclave or their safety, which would they choose? Jacob's words haunted him, predicting the loose affiliations between packs and clans and crews shattering at the slightest pressure from outside. The families in the tunnels had chosen to hide instead of fight. How many still above would choose the same?

They'd been naïve to think it wouldn't come down to a battle between humans and supernaturals. Bearden needed more patrols. Actual fighters, not just the small town police force that mostly carted drunks home or wrote tickets for a misplaced chicken. Delano was bold to attack them, but he wouldn't be the only one to try. The cat was out of the bag and supernaturals were known to the rest of the world. They would need to protect themselves in the future.

If they survived the night.

The hopelessness he saw on faces of neighbors and acquaintances was mirrored more and more on Rylee's. Her scent shifted from determined to downright sad. His bear slashed at him to fix her, to fix everything around them, but Cole could only shove the beast into the back of his mind. There was nothing to be done at that moment.

His eyes floated from face to face, searching for his clan. His alpha brother, preferably, but he'd take the comfort of being near any of them. None were below. He should have known. They wouldn't hide when they could fight. His bear pushed forward again, sending him image after image of soldiers with throats torn out. If the Strathorns were fighting, they needed to be at their side. Defeating their enemies was the best way to keep their mate safe.

One face stood out. "Victor," Cole called over the noise.

The self-proclaimed Vampire King glided into a turn and eyed him coolly. "I didn't expect you to be here with the children, Strathorn."

Cole made a face. "Looking to fix that. The Old Maids said you were the one to talk to."

Victor turned again, gliding around people as he went. "This way, bear."

Victor's throne had been replaced with a large table with a map spread across it. Cole immediately recognized it as Bearden, with all the streets and the tunnels marked out. Victor pointed to a spot outside of town and near the base of the mountains. "The ones that have been caught are being held here." He tapped two other spots. "The nearest tunnel exits are here and here. Fighters are ready to mount a rescue once word gets to the Bloodwings."

"And the rest?"

The murmur of the crowd drowned out Victor's silence, but it still weighed heavily on the small group. "Some have gone into the mountains. Some have gone towards the ranches and towns nearby. Many wanted to stay and fight for our home. Olivia Gale led a small but fierce force until they were overtaken with tranquilizers and silver bullets."

"Did the message get out?" Rylee asked. "They were supposed to find someone, anyone, and raise the alarm about what's happening here."

Victor regarded her for a long moment, then ducked his gaze back to the map. "There has been no word. We might be on our own. Thinking this, a dragon has been dispatched to Wolfden. Many on both sides will be captured or dead before they can arrive."

Jacob shook his head. A note of despair edged his tone. "I'm not going back to that cage. They can't make me go back."

"They won't," Cole told him. "They won't get either of us."

He fixed his eyes on Rylee. He wanted to memorize every detail, from the way her hair hung around her face to the curve of her lips. He had to keep her safe.

Her eyes hardened and she knew what he was going to say even before the words made it to his tongue. She shook her head. "I'm not staying."

"It's safest down here," he reasoned. "You'll have the vampires and all the shifters here."

"I won't have you. I'm not leaving you."

A crack in the distance raised many heads. There was another, then another. Panic clouded the air and filled his nose. Children that'd been calmed started to wail again.

Those continued cracks resolved into distance screams and feet slapping on the ground. The tunnels had been breached.

That decided for him. He wasn't going to leave Rylee to whatever the soldiers had planned. "We need to get out of here." Cole wrapped a hand around Rylee's elbow and pushed her through the crowd toward the tunnels Victor highlighted. Jacob followed on his heels.

The sounds of fighting echoed in the tunnels. No one knew which way to run, and so they scrambled for one exit or another. The hidden sanctuary descended into a writhing, noisy chaos.

He tightened his hold on Rylee as more people

pushed past. Panicked cries and demands stung his sensitive ears while bodies pressed against his little party. He hurried them forward, but the crowd at their backs picked up their pace as the fighting neared.

"This way," he said and ducked into the nearest door leading above. He couldn't risk losing Rylee in the crowd. They could find their way to the fighting from the streets. Better the risk of soldiers than the certainty of being crushed in the press of a panicked mob.

Part of the crowd split off, following him. He urged Rylee and Jacob both in front of him, using his own body as a shield to keep other shifters at bay.

They raced up the stairs and shoved hard at the door leading outside. One push, then another, and the stubborn thing finally scraped open and spilled them into an open clearing. Silence greeted them, sounding loud against the noise coming from behind.

Still, Cole urged Rylee and Jacob to move and make way for those following. The rush to escape wouldn't stop once they hit open air and he wouldn't see her trampled.

The sound of weapons cocking slowed his steps. He raised his hands. On either side, Rylee and Jacob did the same. Fear coated Rylee's scent while pure rage clung to Jacob.

A group of soldiers stood on a rock outcropping above the hidden entrance, ready to capture every soul that spilled out of the opening. One soldier nodded to the others with an ugly glint in his eyes. "Round 'em up and put 'em with the others."

CHAPTER 25

Rylee's heart raced as she eyed the guns pointed at her. A quick glance at her sides showed her Cole and Jacob taking count and considering the situation. Once the men and women in the tunnel realized what trap was springing, they scurried back and slammed the door shut behind them. She couldn't blame them. They were families, most of them, with small children. They couldn't fight and defend those children at the same time.

Twelve soldiers. Maybe four other shifters. She couldn't be sure without twisting around and taking her own count. The soldiers' narrowed eyes and fingers stroking triggers kept her still.

It wasn't Cole or Jacob she needed to worry about. With a wild yell, one of the other shifters jumped forward, a bear ripping out of his body where a man once stood. Two more followed, snarling obscenities and demands to leave Bearden.

Multiple rounds fired. The men yelped and fell to the ground with heavy thuds. The bear latched onto a soldier's arm and shook, hard. It took three more shots before the beast finally slumped into motionlessness.

"Fuck! Fuck! I got bit!" the bitten soldier howled.

Another pointed his weapon at the three unconscious figures. The bear slowly shrunk back down into his human form. "Which one was it?"

"Doesn't matter which one. Only matters if it was an animal." The leader stood from his brief inspection of the bitten one's wounds and everyone took a step back.

The man's eyes went as wide as saucers, his pain forgotten in his fear. "You can't do me like them. You can't! I've been a loyal man from the beginning!" None of the faces softened, and his words pitched higher. "You can't! We don't know if I'll turn into one of them!"

"You have one choice, Rawls. Take it now, or join with your new people."

Rawls swallowed visibly. He pressed his lips

together in a thin line, then walked into the darkness.

Utterly dismissing the wounded man, the leader turned and pointed to the remaining shifters. "You three, pick these ones up."

Weapons stayed trained on them as Cole, Jacob, and the last she didn't know stooped to pick up their fallen brothers. Rylee wanted to shut her eyes and block out the horrid sight of the limp arms and legs, but she forced herself to bear witness.

A soldier jerked his chin toward the closed door. "What about the ones that jumped back inside?"

The leader shrugged. "We know where they are. They'll be smoked out with the rest before the night is over. Good money is being paid for each one we keep alive." He pointed his weapon forward. "Start walking," he ordered.

Behind them, a single crack of gunfire broke through the night. Rylee gasped and turned, but a hand on her shoulder shoved her forward.

"Keep moving," the soldier ordered.

Numb with shock, she put one foot in front of the other.

Did the man have family? Friends that would miss him? He was a monster for going along with the invasion of Bearden, and he certainly deserved punishment for that. She felt pity for him, that his hatred ran so deep that he couldn't accept a new type of existence. She didn't want to be in a world where death was preferable to becoming a shifter.

She didn't know how long they walked. Fifteen minutes, maybe. Definitely through rough terrain that left her winded. She would have kept walking forever if it meant she avoided the detention center.

The soldiers surrounding them marched them into a clearing lit by bright lights and patrolled by more soldiers with more guns. Buses idled nearby in the darkness. Dropping off or picking up, she didn't know.

Too many faces were seated on the ground. Too many hands were bound by glinting cuffs that she knew must be silver. One by one, they perked up and called out names of their friends and family.

Trent. Holly. Gretchen. Connor. Sylvie.

"Becca?" That last came from one of Cole's clan.

The faces of the guards ranged from impassive to hatred. Only a handful looked uncertain, but they weren't stepping forward to help the animals.

Every single thing about it made her sick.

One soldier raised a weapon and shouted as the murmuring of names grew to a roar. "Shut your fucking mouths!"

But the shifters didn't quiet, not until a warning shot was fired over their heads.

She and the others were shoved forward to marks hastily spray painted on the grass. The unconscious shifters were dumped and cuffed, just like the rest of them.

Rylee felt a brief flash of relief when she spotted the rest of the Strathorn clan behind them. Then that relief sunk back into despair. Leah and Hudson were out cold. Callum and the others wore masks of fury. Blood had dried in a long line down Callum's face.

"What happened?" Cole asked quietly over his shoulder.

"Hudson went down after taking out three of theirs. They shot him up with at least four darts. Leah took one meant for me. They've both been out about a half hour now. I don't know what happened to Gideon. He fell from the sky."

"No talking!" The shouting soldier pointed his weapon in their direction.

Rylee fought the urge to cower. The voice, the utter power he exuded, pushed her to obey.

She lifted her chin defiantly. Cole had given her the confidence to stand up for herself. Smart or not, she wasn't going to curl up in fear again. She made her choice to stand by Bearden and some glorified hall monitor with a weapon would not break her with his words alone.

Callum waited until the man moved on. "They might be dressed up and swinging their dicks around, but they're not all soldiers. I overheard one say he wanted a bearskin rug out of this to go with his trophies from Africa."

"Hunters, then. I wouldn't be surprised if Delano handpicked most of the soldiers serving and filled the others' heads with lies before calling in his pals." Jacob flicked his eyes toward Cole. "I told you the enclaves were like lambs to the slaughter."

"Why keep us alive? Why not just put us down now?"

"We're valuable," Callum answered in a harsh whisper. "Prizefighters. They talk about us like we're dogs. The rest, the ones that are hiding, are bait or things to be hunted when they clean up in the next day or two."

Nolan spat. "I'd love to get in the ring with them."

"Easy," Callum ordered. "You saw what they did to Judah and Olivia."

He darted a look to the nearest soldier, then over his shoulder. Rylee saw both with blood smeared across their faces.

"It's not just the tranq darts, either," Callum went on. "Some are loaded up with silver bullets. Half the people here have fragments still in them. No shifting with those under their skin."

"Motherfuckers," Cole growled.

Another soldier passed and waved a gun at them, daring them to keep speaking.

The distant groan of an engine sped her pulse in her chest. More soldiers or more victims, she didn't know which.

The open-doored vehicle pulled to a stop and blocked the path into the clearing. Five soldiers poured out, then stood waiting for the last man to exit.

Major Brant Delano stepped from the vehicle and smiled smugly around his stupid cigar. His cold, dead eyes swept over the crowd and for once, she was glad to see the claw marks on his skin. He deserved that, and more.

"Doc! I should have known you'd be in this shit." Delano puffed out his chest and strut in front of them. "You should have gone back when you had the chance. Now you'll be nothing more than bait for the animals."

A growl rose from Cole, softly at first but steadily building in his chest. Bear he was, and he sounded exactly like a bear warning away a threat that kept pushing closer. She wanted to reach out and touch him. Not to calm him, but to let some of his rage flow through her.

"I couldn't stand by and let these people be hurt."

"But they're not really people," he said with a tone implying she was a simpleton. "That's what you don't get. They might talk like people, they might look like us, hell, they might even fuck like a person. You'd know better than the rest, wouldn't you? Traitor to your own fucking kind." He tucked a finger under her chin and raised her face.

"Get your hands off her!" Cole snapped.

Delano spared him a glance and a sick smile spread across his face when he returned his gaze to Rylee. "Maybe we'll line them up for you. See what comes out at the end of nine months. That's research, isn't it?"

Her heart raced and her hands shook. It was a disgusting, vile idea that had no benefit. It was cruelty. She hated him and all the others willing to go along with his terrible plans.

"Oh ho, this one doesn't like the sound of that!" Delano's face hardened as Cole's growl grew to a fever pitch. "Maybe we'll let you watch."

Cole's eyes turned to pure, liquid gold, and he

tested the strength of the cuffs on his wrists. He rose to his knees, glaring at Delano all the while.

"Sit down," Delano ordered, fingering his sidearm.

"Cole, please," Rylee hurriedly urged. Too much tension thickened the air. Too much could go wrong in a single second. They were better off finding a smart place to take a stand, not creating a situation with too many guns pointed in their direction. "Don't do anything."

Delano swung the butt of his weapon and connected with Cole's temple. "Down, I said," Delano demanded.

"Stop!" Rylee yelled. She struggled to her knees, still screaming the word over and over.

It fell on deaf ears. Delano struck again, then again.

A wave of objections washed over the crowd. She hated the way Delano only grinned wider. He liked causing pain, and he wanted everyone to see how much of a hard ass he could be. It made her skin crawl.

"You animals will learn who your masters are," Delano snarled.

Soft rustles of movement behind her stole her attention from Delano's intimidation theatrics. One by one, heads cocked to catch a noise in the distance. The soldiers glanced at one another with a mixture of confusion and worry on their faces. Fingers tightened around their weapons and adjusted their protection in their arms.

She caught the noise at the same time as the other humans. The chopping of blades through the air that signaled helicopters. Friends or foes? She slid a look to Delano, but couldn't read his reaction. He didn't know, either.

The first blinking lights appeared in the distance and Delano yelled to his men. "Get them loaded on the busses! Now!"

The lines furthest back were the ones first jerked to their feet. Rylee knew enough of history that no good would come from stepping on those busses.

A struggle started almost from the beginning. Rylee glanced over her shoulder, then back to the lights in the sky. Faster, she urged. Please be help.

The first line of shifters dug in their heels and refused to move. Multiple soldiers grabbed hold of arms and legs and tried to drag the resisting offenders into the darkness. Even bound and shot, they wouldn't give in easily.

Still other soldiers murmured uneasily. Those were the ones playing dress up, just as Callum said.

They weren't real fighters. They didn't have the training to put down a growing, growling rebellion.

She prayed help would arrive before the nervous ones started shooting.

The second line was forced to their feet before the first even moved into the darkness beyond the clearing. More resistance came from even more unwilling shifters. There weren't enough hands to drag them forward.

Spotlights brightened the clearing and Rylee tore her gaze away from the struggle behind her. Four helicopters hovered over the clearing, with more circling around the scene.

She held her breath. Friend or foe?

"Drop your weapons and put your hands behind your heads!"

Rylee nearly collapsed to her hands with relief. Someone heard their message. Help had come to Bearden.

But an eerie quiet settled over the clearing. It was loud, even over the helicopters. Everyone waited for something. Some signal to fight or kill. Some sign that the entire ordeal was over.

Tension grew the longer Delano stayed silent. He glanced at his men surrounding the captured citizens of Bearden. One tiny hand gesture was all it took for them to raise their weapons toward the helicopters. The crews in the sky responded by drawing weapons of their own.

In that confusion, Rylee's cuffs bit into her wrists and she was hauled to her feet. The stench of Delano's cigar and sweat curdled her stomach. And something hard pressed against the base of her skull.

"I'm walking out of here, or she gets a bullet to the back of her head!"

Coward. Yellow-bellied weasel. Terrorist. He couldn't put down his weapon and accept he'd been caught ready to sell Bearden into slavery and death. He had to take everyone to hell with him.

This was how she died. Even if both sides took extreme care, the firefight would surely stray into the innocent crowd.

She accepted it. Internalized it. And met Cole's eyes for the final seconds of her life.

At least she'd known him. At least she started to heal. He helped with that process, and she had so much gratitude and love for him. Finding people who could change into ferocious beasts and getting close to a man again seemed like equally far off possibilities before she journeyed to Bearden, but Cole filled both roles. He'd taken a weak, damaged girl and given her the strength and courage to face death on her feet.

But he wasn't about to let her go so easily.

Cole surged to his feet with a feral challenge on his lips and ripped her out of Delano's grasp. With a quick twist of his body, he placed himself between her and the madman.

A crack of gunfire reached her ears just as Cole stiffened.

Chaos and confusion erupted all around. Small groups banded together and targeted soldiers. Still others grabbed children and ran for the tree line.

For every person who ran, more streamed into the clearing. Backup had arrived and worked with the humans trying to put down Delano's hateful mission. Partial and full shifts struck against guns. Real bullets, not just tranquilizers, fired into the attack and more bodies fell to the ground.

Then a roar pierced the night, followed closely by another. A jet of fire shot into the air. Trees shook and bent until they broke. Two dragon heads broke into the clearing, halting the escape of some soldiers.

Ropes dropped from the helicopters. The low whizz of cord passing through gloves preceded bodies thunking down to the ground.

Rylee ignored it all. She leaned over Cole and

pressed her hands over his heart. "No, no, no," she muttered over and over.

There was a limit to shifter healing, and she feared she'd found it.

Blood seeped out of the wound that didn't look like it was closing in the slightest.

Cole sucked in a quick breath and his eyes snapped open. "Let me up," he wheezed. "Need to shift."

"You've been shot!"

"Need to shift!" He jackknifed upward, then tugged the cuffs on his wrists as far apart as he could manage. "Need keys or to break these off."

Good Lord, his voice sounded too raspy. Syllables dropped out of his words, like there wasn't enough air in his lungs to push past his vocal cords. His face was drawn and ashen and terrifying.

She moved even before her mind could process what she was doing. The Strathorns were with her, hauling Delano to the ground. She didn't care who made the killing blow or how. She just needed in his pockets.

"Keys, keys, keys," she chanted, diving into one and then the next. Four pockets and an eternity later, her fingers brushed against cool metal.

Then she threw herself back to Cole.

He'd managed to rip one cuff off his wrist. It pained her to look at the broken fingers and raw skin on his hand from scraping metal over himself. She nearly had to pin him to the ground to insert the key into the hole on the remaining cuff. He shoved her away as soon as the metal fell from his hand.

His mouth stretched open, and a roar tore out of his throat.

CHAPTER 26

For two long days, Cole was kept hostage in his own bed by a woman who could barely reach his shoulders. She was the gatekeeper to his home and harsh mistress of his diet. He doubted he could sneak past her if he even tried.

"Rylee, please," he laughed and tried to pull his arms out from the blanket she insisted on tucking around him. It was more like a straight jacket than a comforter.

She pursed her lips and adjusted her glasses. "You need to rest."

"I'm healed. Look!" Cole threw back the blankets she'd just tucked around him. A tiny, pink pucker marred his chest just below his heart. He had worse marks from his last brawl with the clan.

He thought he won when her eyes darkened and her breath hitched in her chest. Wildflowers and fresh rain filled the air, slowly thickening as her blood heated to a simmer. A growl worked its way out of his chest, low enough that she couldn't hear. The thought of her wanting him turned him on.

Two fucking days with her constantly hovering nearby was pure torture when she wouldn't let him touch her. And sure, he'd been pretty weak those first twelve hours after his shift, but that mostly passed after a good sleep and breakfast. He was getting antsy in bed and unable to do anything but stare at the ceiling. His bear wanted out. No, that wasn't right. The beast wanted Rylee.

Mate.

Cole's growl took on a new pitch of contentment.

"You could still have a fragment inside," she insisted. "Or a tear to the muscle. You lost so much blood and there's very little known about your healing abilities."

"I shifted, didn't I? Which means no fragments—"

"No *silver* fragments," she interrupted.

He hated even thinking about that entire fucking day. Beaten, seemingly betrayed, then captured again. A rollercoaster of emotion was entirely too accurate. He could have lost her so easily at multiple points.

At least they'd won. The message she'd worked to get to the outside summoned a force ready to take down Delano and his disgusting friends. The war wasn't over by a long shot, but they'd managed to win one battle.

He had another fight to win. He didn't care how many skirmishes it took. Rylee would be his mate. He'd claim her just as soon as she gave the word. He didn't care if she wanted to stay human or asked for a bear. He simply needed her heart.

"I'm healed, Rylee. You're stuck with me now. No shuffling me off the mortal coil. You'll have to do better if you're leaving me."

"I am not leaving—" She snapped her mouth shut and shook a finger at him. "No changing the subject. I want to do an ultrasound to make sure you aren't bleeding internally."

Cole rolled his eyes and sat up. She tried to push him back into bed, but he set his feet on the ground. Standing up to his full height dragged her to her feet with him. He managed one step before she wrapped herself around him like an octopus.

They crashed to the floor in a jumble of limbs. Cole turned to take the brunt of the fall. Maybe on purpose. Maybe so she'd spill over his chest. His eyes nearly rolled to the back of his head when he felt the faintest trace of her heat against his groin.

Two long fucking days.

Rylee propped herself on her elbows and stared down at him with those big blue eyes he loved. "You could have died."

"I will die, one day."

Her eyes narrowed. "Don't talk like that!"

"It's part of life. We're not immortal like the vamps." She opened her mouth to object, and he hushed her. "Okay, okay. I didn't die, and I will not die from this. If something was wrong, we'd know by now."

She rolled her shoulders and released a fraction of the tension she carried. "You're sure you feel fine? I'd still like to have a doctor look at you."

"I have a hot one looking at me right now." She growled at him. Growled! He struggled to keep his laugh contained. "I'm fine. Wounds and fights are part of being a shifter."

He leaned up and caught her in a slow, simmering kiss. The scent of wildflowers exploded around him and he laid bare his soul. "I'm going to spend every second I have left in this world worshipping the ground you walk on. I hated needing to watch you when you came here, and now I can't imagine doing anything else. You make me a better person, Rylee. You calm my bear when I need it, challenge me when I'm being stubborn. I didn't think I had a mate, and you proved me wrong. There are some scary big changes coming for us all, you included if you stay, but I'm ready for them if I have you at my side."

It was a good speech if he had to be the judge. But it was for her and only her opinion mattered.

Her eyes softened when he met them, and she leaned forward. Cole skimmed his hands up her back and settled one in her hair and the other against her cheek. She felt so good to touch, and even better to kiss.

He sipped at her lips slowly. Deliberately. Giving her every chance to pull back, just like the first time he pressed his lips to hers. Each second she didn't step back tied him more firmly to his decision. She belonged with him. He'd follow her to the ends of the earth. Air to breathe, food to eat, none of that mattered if he didn't have Rylee.

"I know we talked about seeing where this goes. But Cole... You took a bullet meant for me. You could have died! And I don't want that to happen before I... before we..." Her nostrils flared with a frustrated breath. A hint of red spread across her cheeks. "I want to be mated to you."

He'd felt happiness and joy before, but nothing to the degree that unfurled in his chest with those words. He flipped them over, scenting for any trace of fear that might remain. Nothing. Only excitement and wildflowers greeted his nose.

Bear shoving forward, he ran his mouth up the column of her neck. "Say it again."

Her voice turned breathy. "I want you to mate me and I don't want you to hold back."

Cole pulled back and studied her face. His cock strained against his sweatpants. It was everything he could do not to bury himself inside her that very moment. "What do you mean?"

"I mean..." she trailed off, chewing on her lip. "You've been gentle with me. Careful. And you don't need to, not anymore."

He dragged his fingers down her arms, raising goose bumps as he went. Running out of arm, he wrapped his fingers around her wrists and pulled them over her head. "You want me to fuck you, is that what you're saying? You want me to be rougher?"

A slight tug was all it took for him to release one

of her hands. She cupped his cheek and kissed him lightly. "I trust you."

Two long, horrible, worrying days and finally it was over. He was back on his feet. Or rather, off them. In good health. He was better and—

Rylee's thoughts vanished into thin air the moment Cole slid his hand under her top. He palmed her breast through her bra before clever fingers inched the lacy material out of the way.

"Tease," she breathed.

A growl eased out of his chest and he moved quickly, shoving the hem up over her waist and chest. He tugged and pulled and trapped her wrists in her shirt, then bent back to her breast.

Rylee arched into him the moment his lips closed around her nipple. He tongued and sucked until it was a stiff peak. He cupped her other breast, teasing and thumbing until that, too, was a hardened nub.

Freeing her hands, she trailed them down his body. So strong. Packed with power. And now all hers.

That was a jolt to her system on par with the hard rock of Cole's hips right where she wanted him. Hers. Mating was a serious commitment. For life. And he chose her. One tiny, damaged human laid claim to the big bad bear. She felt like she could take on the world with him at her back.

Rylee pressed her palm to Cole's shaft, squeezing as she slid up and down. She adored the feel of him. Loved how his hips jerked against her hand. Delighted in the groan that caught in the back of his throat.

Power. That's what she had with him. Just as much power as he had over her.

His hand slipped down her bare stomach and plunged into her panties. He zeroed in on her at once, driving a finger straight into her center.

"Mine," he said, voice full of sexy gravel. His eyes were pure gold as he watched the reactions he drew from her.

She couldn't manage any sound but a throaty moan. She chased his hand on every retreat, seeking more of the pleasure that blossomed in her core. He had her right on the edge of bliss with a searing hot look and fingers that knew exactly where to touch.

"More," she pleaded.

She caught his nostrils flaring. Testing for any hesitation, she assumed. And when he found none, he dipped his head back to her chest. His teeth scraped gently over her nipple. Then he moved again, trailing fire and kisses down her navel.

His fingers slipped from her and she cursed softly. "You'll have to do better than that, little bit," Cole teased.

He made quick work of the button and zipper of her jeans, then pulled them down her legs so fast she thought they were ripped away.

He lifted her and eased her back on the bed. His eyes roved over her body and she saw herself through them. Flushed cheeks, messed hair, bra askance and pushing her breasts higher. Heat and utter need darkened his gaze.

Her bad bear wouldn't be held back much longer. Rylee pressed her thighs together to hold back a shiver of excitement.

Wise mistake. Cole's golden eyes grazed down her body and another growl pooled more heat in her core.

He dipped his head between her legs, shoulders pushing her thighs apart. Her panties snapped, and he attacked with his mouth.

"Fuck," she hissed. A dark chuckle was the only sign that he'd heard her.

Cole's fingers returned, spearing her and curling inside. He made it his mission to turn her every breath ragged and harsh. He sucked and tongued, stroked and plunged.

Her world reduced down entirely to him and his worship. There was no other word for it. Her pleasure brought his own. His groans sprang to life on the heels of her moans. She arched and writhed, and he feasted.

Rylee threw back her head. His name burned her lips and fire burned through her veins.

Then he was on her, sliding home with a hoarse growl. He rode through her orgasm, breath beating out of his lungs. He filled her in one solid thrust, pressing all around her, taking up a spot in every cell of her being.

One thrust, two. He held himself up on his hands, giving her space and being gentle. Careful. Testing her limits. Rylee wrapped her arms around his neck and drew him down to her. She'd been serious before. She trusted him with her life. She didn't want him to hold back.

"Harder," she groaned into his ear.

His hips rocked into her, but then he restrained himself again. He skimmed a trail of hot, sucking kisses up her throat and across her jaw. "You don't smell afraid," he growled into her mouth.

"You wouldn't hurt me. Don't hold back anything

from me. I'm yours." She chased his lips into a heated kiss. She pushed her tongue past his lips and rolled her hips, meeting him stroke for stroke everywhere they were connected.

Cole's eyes glowed a brighter gold with the last bit of hesitation dropping away. "Mine," he growled again and thrust harder into her.

Rylee gasped as he drove his cock deeper. Each drag of skin filled her with a longing he immediately solved. His fingers dug into her hips and held her in place. His thrusts sped up, gliding against her in shorter, rougher bursts that made stars appear behind her eyes. She dragged her nails down his arms and back, looking for something to hold on as he turned her world inside out.

His eyes found her and locked her in his gaze. Need and desire circled there, right along with possession. She belonged to him, utterly and entirely. She was bound to him completely and he hadn't yet put his fangs in her skin.

And as he took her, he gave himself.

"Say it. Say the words."

His words rough and raspy and sent liquid heat spilling inside her. "I love you, Cole Strathorn. I love you, I love you, I love you."

He gathered her into his arms, eyes still meeting

hers. She could feel eternity there, just behind his lids. Eternity with Cole. That was the most perfect idea ever thought into existence.

"Yours," he growled against her lips. Then his mouth was gone, and he kissed a line straight to her shoulder.

He slammed into her again and again, hips jerking and losing that perfect rhythm. Pleasure and emotion twined together and tied them together.

"Yours," he murmured against her skin.

Her whole body shook. Now. It had to be now. Right on the cusp of another shattering orgasm, right before her mind slipped away from her, Cole sank fangs into her shoulder and thrust one final time into her.

Rylee cried out from the total pleasure overload. She dug her fingers into his hair. She felt raw and needed to tether herself to something, to him.

She didn't know how long they stayed wrapped up in each other's arms. It was impossible to care. She had her mate and a peace she never thought possible after years of pain.

With light kisses, Cole pulled from her and tucked her against his side. She loved this hidden side of him. The need to touch after. She'd grown insecure before and thrown on one of his shirts.

Now, though... she wanted his eyes and hands and mouth on her. They belonged to each other.

A grin spread across her face. "You'll need to meet my mother and siblings. I'm sure they'll want to meet the man that stole my heart."

Cole snorted. "I'd rather be shot again."

He dodged her first playful slap and caught her second. A cocked eyebrow and fingers rough from hard labor running over the fresh claiming mark on her shoulder were enough to distract her from thoughts of anything but staying forever in their bed.

EPILOGUE

"...And in further revelations, the investigations into Major Brant Delano's actions in Bearden have led to three more enclaves stepping out of the shadows. With more supernaturals revealing themselves every day, one must wonder at the incredible lack of foresight in this attack on United States citizens. This is Arabella Hocking, continuing your coverage of what some are calling Shifter-gate. Tune in tomorrow for the latest breakdown of the subcommittee's proceedings."

Rylee reached for the remote and flicked off the television mounted to the wall. She'd avoided watching most of the seemingly endless hearings on exactly how Delano was able to pull off his incursion into the Bearden enclave, but she still liked to catch a summary at the end of the day. And when nothing new was ready to be reported, Arabella Hocking liked to air pieces on the citizens of Bearden. More than a few had stepped forward, despite an early resistance. Someone put a bug in their ear that showing off regular life would make them sympathetic figures in the media.

It was a good strategy. The number of protesters outside the enclave dwindled every day, while the number of those toting signs of support grew. The coverage that painted Delano as a rogue commander certainly helped, too.

Her part in the narrative wasn't over, either. She'd been flown out to D.C. to give her testimony, then shipped back to her home lab in Nevada to meet with the supervisors there. That was when she was offered a dream come true: stay in Bearden and manage the needs of research teams with the goal of understanding and spreading knowledge of the supernatural residents. She had the trust of the town, it was argued, and what she lacked in management experience could be solved with a plethora of resources at her fingertips.

She was under no illusions. Her silence was being bought, but it was a price she was willing to pay.

Besides, the clearly stated goal of understanding and showing the supernaturals were no bigger threat than a neighbor across the street was what she wanted in the first place. Now she had some very public guarantees that no harm would be done.

Leaving Bearden was never an option. Cole was there, and she couldn't leave her mate.

Absently, her fingers ran over the mark under her shirt. Just thinking about the man drifted her into blisteringly hot daydreams. The response was even more powerful when her bad bear walked into the empty lab.

His eyes slid to her fingers tracing the mark. Heated gold simmered there when he jerked his gaze to her face. "We can be late," he said thickly.

Rylee yanked her hand away and stood quickly, chair scraping against the floor. She kept the table between them. "We cannot be late. People will notice if we keep showing up late for everything."

Lunch, work, dinner, coffee, brunch, and runs in the woods were all examples of tardiness just that week. She nearly missed her plane to Nevada on her last summoned meeting. The man was insatiable, and she loved it even if she complained.

Cole was around the table faster than she could track. She was almost willing to let him give her a bear of her own just to watch him move. But that was on the backburner, at least until she had her new teams up and running. Taking time off to manage an unruly new beast wasn't in the cards.

Rylee's back hit the wall. Cole's thumbs rubbed slow circles against her hips while his lips traveled a hot journey down her neck. "You smell like wildflowers, little bit. I bet I could have you screaming in five minutes."

Heat curled in her center and her heart picked up speed. Then his lips met the top line of her mate mark and any resistance vanished. "Make it two and we have a deal," she breathed, hands already winding around his neck.

CHAIRS LINED up in perfect rows nearly filled the town square, and even those weren't enough to contain all the people that planned to attend the Mayor's opening ceremony. Bearden residents that couldn't find and claim a seat lingered at the sides or in the streets hugging the square, some waiting patiently for the remarks to be over while others hurriedly finished prepping street stalls for the celebration.

Coming together was something they all needed, Cole explained. Not only did the individual packs and clans and crews need to seek comfort in one another, but the town needed it to heal. So a small carnival was planned, with food and games and drinking and dancing to bind the town back together after needing to defend themselves.

A platform had been raised at one end of the square. Pictures of every Bearden life lost during Delano's attack were displayed for all to see. Too many faces, in her opinion, but even one would have been too many for her bleeding heart.

Callum led the Strathorns to the second row, where Nolan and Sawyer were sprawled out and saving seats for the entire clan. The front row was marked with printed signs proclaiming the names of honored guests. People milled around, shaking hands and slapping backs with the air of importance. Always thinking of her, Cole claimed the seats at the end of the row, leaving her the chair along the aisle.

Rylee pointed when she spotted the mayor's assistant walking across the platform. It took a few minutes more before everyone found a seat. Only when a murmured hush fell over the crowd did Olivia Gale stand and make her way to the microphone.

"Spring is a time for growth and renewal. I've thought long and hard about the words I wanted to say today, and those words kept coming back to me. Every year, regardless of whether we've been inside an enclave or out, we've seen spring spread green over wintery lands. And that's what I choose to focus on when I think about what has changed in a few short months. We have been forced to grow. We have been forced to show ourselves to the world. And we will thrive."

A smattering of claps grew and grew. Olivia herself led a small team against Delano's men. They'd saved and pushed dozens of families with small children down into the tunnels or into the mountains before they were overwhelmed.

Her story wasn't the only one Rylee had heard over the weeks. Everyone seemed to have a story of helping someone out or making sure someone was safe. Judah and his police force, the ranchers on the outskirts of town, the Strathorns, even the Holden sisters all came up as heroes and heroines willing to fight for their home.

Bearden wasn't just a place for them. Bearden was family and friends and lives. That dedication to one another misted Rylee's eyes every time she thought about it.

"I'd like to thank the Wolfden, Ruin's Edge, and Firebend enclaves for stepping forward as soon as they heard of our need. They stood up in the face of danger and added their voices to the cause of our collective survival. It would have been too easy to watch Bearden's destruction and keep their own lives hidden. We cannot be destroyed if others are willing to raise the alarm. Thank you." Olivia nodded to the leaders of the enclaves and favored them with a smile.

"I'd also like to extend a special thanks to the newest member of our community, and one with a great heart. With her whole world crashing down around her, she fought to keep us all alive. Everyone, please give our own Doctor Rylee Garland a brief round of applause."

A flush grew on Rylee's cheeks. She smiled and gave the crowd around her a tiny wave before ducking her face into Cole's shoulder. "Was this you?"

"Not at all." He squeezed her thigh. "You deserve it, though. Brave, perfect mate."

"I didn't do anything special," she protested.

"You went out of your way, putting yourself in danger, to hold off someone perfecting ways to kill us. Pretty fucking special." Cole lifted her chin and gave her a quick kiss. The applause around them turned to oohs and awws and Rylee dashed tears away from the corner of her eyes.

She'd found her place in the world.

The rest of the ceremony concluded with a moment of silence for all the fallen. More than one set of eyes were wet when the crowd was released into happier activities.

She found herself grouped together with the rest of the Strathorns near the Mug Shot and Tommy's Diner stalls nestled right next to each other. Leah was mercilessly teasing and challenging the others to games of shot glass ring toss, as she called it, demanding everyone take a shot before attempting to throw a ring over hooks. It was going as terrible as possible and Rylee could barely stand straight for laughing.

A round man with red cheeks toddled toward her. "Donal and Honora Conri," Cole whispered quickly. "Leaders of the Conri pack and Wolfden."

"Doctor Garland, what a pleasure to meet you!" Donal exclaimed. Honora gave her a tiny, practiced smile.

"Thank you," she said, holding out her hand. She stiffened slightly when he bent over and planted a kiss on the back.

"You must come to our annual ball. We have discussed the subject, and will open our enclave to your researchers."

"Oh, that's wonderful! Thank you. That's just... There's a whole list of questions I'd like to ask whenever you have a moment. When and where and what you'd like me to do or not do." Rylee snapped her mouth shut, realizing she was letting her words get away with her. She dipped her chin and said as gracefully as possible, "This is a great honor."

Honora nodded. "Please, forward all your questions to our son, Finn. He will arrange everything."

"A ball?" Rylee's eyes widened as soon as Donal and Honora disappeared into the crowd.

Tommy glared after the Conri leaders. "Sounds as ridiculous as it is. They play dress up and wear masks, as if they can't smell who each other are underneath. There's food and dancing all night, then a big fireworks show at the stroke of midnight."

"Don't mind Tommy," Faith said as she stood on her toes and kissed his cheek. "He's just upset that as a Conri in disgrace that he's no longer invited."

"I am not in disgrace," he said stiffly.

"You mated a fox. Those pureblood Conri genes are going to waste," Faith teased. "I wouldn't have it any other way."

She gave him another smile and Rylee could feel her heart melting. She probably looked like that when she even thought about Cole.

Rylee bumped her shoulder against her own mate. "You'll need a tux."

Cole frowned. "Not a fucking chance."

"I don't know... A tattooed bad boy, all cleaned up? That sounds pretty delicious."

He grabbed her wrist and started toward the edge of the square. "Cole!" she laughed. "Where are we going?"

He threw a glance over his shoulder. "We can probably throw a rock through the formal wear shop and nab something while everyone is distracted."

Rylee laughed, aghast, but let her bear lead her away. She could always pay for any damage later if he was truly serious.

ABOUT THE AUTHOR

Cecilia Lane grew up in a what most call paradise, but she insists is humid hell. She escaped the heat with weekly journeys to the library, where she learned the basics of slaying dragons, magical abilities, and grand adventures.

When it became apparent she wouldn't be able to travel the high seas with princes or party with rock star vampires, Cecilia hunkered down to create her own worlds filled with sexy people in complicated situations. She now writes with the support of her own sexy man and many interruptions from her goofy dog.

Connect with Cecilia online!
www.cecilialane.com

Made in the USA
Middletown, DE
25 September 2021